The Road Home

Elvish Chronicles, Volume 2

Prudence MacLeod

Published by Prudence MacLeod, 2024.

The Road Home

(second edition)

by

Prudence MacLeod

Copyright July 2016

THE ROAD HOME

First edition. March 19, 2024.

Copyright © 2024 Prudence MacLeod.

ISBN: 978-1927478752

Written by Prudence MacLeod.

In this, the second chronicle of the Elves of Elendor, I will relate some of the trials and dangers faced by the Elves as Queen Ariel led them to a new home in the haunted forests of the north. Many were the dangers and rogue magics that had to be overcome on that long trek across the mountains, and many were the heroes who rose to face them.

The Long Chain of Fire

Ariel, Queen of the Elves, sat on her charger and gazed at the long string of people slowly making their way along the forest trail. The numbers of Elves seemed endless as they passed before her eyes. Only now was she beginning to understand the magnitude of the task she'd set for herself.

Beside her sat her companion, a centuries old warrior, an assassin without equal. The warrior had known, of course. From the first moment she'd seen Ariel asleep on that rooftop, she had known what lay ahead. "Well, my delight, are you pleased?"

"I'm terrified, Mearith, my heart. My only thought has been to set them free, but now I begin to see the magnitude of the task before me. Only now do I begin to see what I've done to them."

"Done to them? By setting them free?"

"Look at them, my heart. So many of them are terrified, and they're in no fit condition for this journey. The air will soon grow cold, and we have no cloaks or boots for them, no weapons either. How are we ever to get them over the mountains in winter?"

"Well, it's not winter yet. With luck, we'll escape that fate and be in Narthwood before the snows catch us."

"Do you truly believe that?"

"No, I don't. However, I believe someone else may have anticipated some of our needs."

"Oh?"

"Dear heart, Evanseth's greatest strength has always been his ability to see the upcoming obstacles, and to prepare for them. I think it's time we sent out some runners and scouts. We need news of what lies ahead, and we need news of Fugitive.

"If I know Evan he'll have left supplies for us at Fugitive, at least as much as he could spare. We need to know what's there and how much more we need to acquire before we reach the mountains."

Ariel nodded, deep in thought as the seemingly endless chain of Elves passed before her eyes. "As usual you've seen what I didn't and have taken the appropriate steps to prepare. I'd be so lost without you, my heart. You should have been the one to be queen, the one to lead us to freedom."

"No, my delight, you're the queen. You're the one with the vision, the ability to inspire all to your cause. Under my leadership, they would falter, the dream would fail, and all would pass away into the mystery of time.

"Ariel, my queen, my heart, it's you and you alone who can lead the Elves to freedom, bring us all back from the brink."

"I do hope your faith in me isn't misplaced."

"It isn't, have no fear. Ariel, may I ask something?"

"Of course."

"When you sent L'ark to seek out his companion's daughter, you seemed to feel quite strongly about that. Could you tell me about it?"

Ariel sighed then straightened in the saddle. "Tereen was ever a second mother to me. Telee and I were inseparable as children. We often played a game of freeing the slaves. We swore that we would both find a path to freedom and the first to achieve that would seek out and buy the other so we could both be free.

"Master overheard us talking about it one day, and I got the beating of my life. It was explained to me, at the business end of a whip, that I was an Elf, a slave, born to obey, to be owned. I was forbidden to see them ever again or they would be bought and killed before my eyes."

"But you didn't forget your vow to free your friend."

"Not for a single moment. Do you think L'ark will succeed?"

Mearith grinned. "He will succeed, my delight. Both L'ark and his brother L'mak are of the Southern Clans, no more tenacious creature exists. You may yet meet your childhood friend on the road to Narthwood."

"I do hope you're right. Come, let's find the end of the line and make sure everything is well there."

"I'll go. The queen should ride at the head of the column." With that, Mearith leaned towards Ariel, kissed her cheek, and then trotted off towards the end of the line. Ariel turned her eyes forward and set out.

As she reached the front of the line she found her general waiting for her with her personal guard. "Arlon, why have we stopped?"

"The day grows late, my queen," replied the general. "The way ahead is difficult, and the people are tired. I thought it best to face the rocky terrain ahead after they've rested and eaten."

Ariel nodded and dismounted. "That's good thinking, my friend. Make it so. Tanis."

"Yes, my queen?"

"You were scouting towards the open roads."

"I was, yes."

"What news?"

"The roads are empty, my queen."

"Empty?"

"Yes, my queen, nothing moved, no horse, wagon, or traveler, could be seen."

She stripped the saddle from the horse's back and pulled up a handful of sweet grass. She began to rub him down and he nickered his delight. "Arlon, Tanis, advise me now. If we could travel the road, even for a single day, we would avoid the rocky terrain ahead and gain a great deal of speed. What think you?"

"Well, you're absolutely right about the speed and distance, Lady," replied Arlon. "It'll take all day to cross the rocky hill ahead, with a gain of less than half a league. By taking to the roads we could manage two leagues in the same amount of time."

"Could it be a trap? Could there be an army in hiding, just waiting for us?"

"Possible, I suppose," replied Arlon, "but I doubt it. The only place to hide an army hereabouts is in the edge of the forest. We would know if they were here."

"Unless they were on the other side of the road," grinned Tanis.

Arlon clapped a hand on his shoulder. "Yes, my young friend, unless they were on the other side of the road."

Ariel smiled at them both. "What do you think, Arlon, is it worth a look?"

"Oh yes, my queen, it is indeed worth a look."

"Tanis."

"My queen?"

"Why are you still here?"

"I'm already gone, Lady," he called over his shoulder as he sped away, the rest of the guard falling into step behind him. They could run free for a while, with an army around her, the queen would be quite safe.

Mearith returned to her as the campfires were lit and food prepared. All the Elves had passed through the awakening and now, as they took their rest after a day of travel, they relaxed back to listen to the voices of the forest.

As darkness fell, Ariel climbed to a vantage point and looked back along the trail. Many of the campfires were visible to her, but not from the road below them. "What troubles you, Mearith, my love?"

"It's like a chain of fire," she replied, as she too gazed at the long line of campfires. "Invisible from the road below, but the light cast by the chain is not. If anyone bothers to take notice it wouldn't be so hard to puzzle out."

"I can't ask them to go without the basic warmth of fire. At least not until we get them better clothing and warm cloaks."

"I know, my delight, I know. They've not been off the Oshar long enough for their bodies to naturally generate the necessary heat. You or I could easily go weeks without cloaks or fire at this time of year, but not these poor people."

"Is there nothing we can do for them?" asked Ariel. "I was fortunate enough to have you to help and guide me. Most of these folk have no one."

They gazed at the chain of fires for a few moments then Ariel spoke again. "Mearith, what do you estimate our numbers to be?"

"Our numbers?"

"Newly freed to Borni, what is the ratio, do you think?"

"We have about fifteen hundred Borni, with nearly a thousand newly freed to care for, roughly speaking. What do you have in mind?"

"As I said before, I had you to guide me. Consider this, each newly freed could be assigned a Borni warrior to be a guide and mentor for the journey to Elfhome. The guide could teach language, wood craft, and fighting skills while on the journey, as well as provide assistance at time of need.

"That would still leave five hundred Borni to act guards, scouts, hunters, and protectors on the journey. The newly freed would still be part of the greater group, but have a special guide as well. What do you think?"

"My queen, how I do love the way your mind works. I'd never have thought of that, but it's an idea with great merit. I like it. Shall we run it past Arlon and Trelanth?"

"Let's do," grinned Ariel.

The general and the mage listened attentively while the queen outlined her idea. They both nodded in agreement. "Several have already been chosen by the Spiritpull," said Trelanth. "Those would be natural pairs."

"Agreed," said Arlon. "Actually, I like it, my queen. We'll be able to travel faster this way and lose fewer folk along the trail. The only problem I can foresee is if we meet heavy opposition. Most of our troops would be hampered until the newly freed could be moved back out of harm's way."

"Tell me truly now, Arlon, are we likely to meet such opposition in the forest?"

"No, Lady, we're not. Only when we're on the open road could we be so confronted."

Ariel sat lost in thought for a while, staring into the fire. Finally, she looked up again. "Mearith, tell me of the way ahead. If we abandon the trees for a day we can get around the cliffs ahead. From there could we continue on the other side of the road, or should we return to this side?"

"Once around the cliffs it would be best to return to this side for a time. Should we cross too soon we could be pushed against the great swamps that protect the privacy of Fugitive.

"At our current rate of travel, we need a day to pass the cliffs, and eight more until we reach the best place to cross. If we can use the road to skirt around the cliffs we can cut one day at least off that timeline."

Ariel's eyes suddenly hardened. "And if we took to the roads and marched there on to the crossing place?"

Mearith met her gaze squarely. "That would take only three days in total. However, all stealth would be lost. The ruse of us heading south would be lost. The Geni would know where to find us, even if we made it back into the forest.

"They could then oppose us in the mountains, especially near the ruins of Elanda, the place where the High Born fell. There is still much old and twisted magic resting there in the broken places of the palace grounds."

"We need to move with greater haste," sighed Ariel. "We watched from the trees as over a thousand men at arms rode south. I believe the ruse worked and they have sent all they have to spare to capture us.

"Trelanth, what think you? Is it worth the risk?"

"That I cannot say, my Lady, but this I do know. Many who journey with us now will not survive if winter catches us in the mountain reaches."

"Mearith?"

"She speaks truly, my delight."

"Your opinion?"

Mearith sighed then spoke. "We should take the risk. It's a gamble, but we're running out of time and alternatives."

"Then we await the return of Tanis. If he reports the roads empty of travelers, then we take to the roads. Arlon, see that every newly freed is assigned a warrior to mentor, teach, and protect." He nodded then rose and moved away to the next campfire.

The night was well along when that task was completed. All along the chain of fire the warriors approached and introduced themselves. They spoke for only a moment then covered their new charges with their own cloaks before settling down to sleep.

They were all awake before the sun arose the next morning. Everyone was making a meal of cold rations while awaiting the return of Tanis. Seeing the queen was awake, Arlon approached.

"It's done?" she asked.

"It's done, my queen," he replied. "We've tried to pair them as best possible. The strongest were paired with the weak and the mothers with children close, those who didn't go through to Sanctuary. The most likely warriors were paired with the most adept at weapons, and so it goes.

"I've done my best, my queen, but in truth, many who should be here to mentor are with the king."

"It's all right, Arlon, you've done well and put more thought into it than I had. Thank you for that."

At that point Korath, a member of her guard, came trotting into the camp and dropped to one knee before Ariel. "I bring news, my queen."

Ariel smiled at her earnest young guardsman. "Rise, Korath, and share the news."

He was grinning with delight. "Lady, when we reached the road last night we heard people approaching. It was twenty soldiers herding a hundred slaves along, headed for Magdan, replacements for some of those we freed.

"We slipped in close to their camp and listened. Lady, most able-bodied soldiers and sell swords have gone south to hunt us. Shotar has retained barely enough to guard the city. All merchants and travelers have been warned to stay off the roads."

"That is welcome news indeed, Korath," said Ariel as she gripped his shoulder tight, "but what of the slaves you saw?"

"Tanis should be here with them in a few minutes, my queen." He was grinning with delight.

"And what of the soldiers who guarded them?" asked Mearith.

"The bodies have been dragged into the trees and hidden, Lady. The oshar they carried in a wagon was dumped out and the wagon left in the trees as well. The horses now carry the food, weapons, and clothing of the soldiers."

Ariel laughed with delight. A moment later Tanis arrived with his new charges. They were soon integrated with the rest of the group. Arlon wasn't smiling now.

"Arlon?"

"Forgive me, Lady Ariel, the boy did right, to be sure, but we now have a hundred fewer warriors to guard our passage. Are we still going to risk the roads?"

"We are."

"Then may I suggest Trelanth and her mages reach the road first and leave it last?"

"That is precisely what we had in mind," smiled Trelanth, as she and her fellow mages approached.

"Then let's get moving," said Ariel, as she threw the saddle on Grimm's back. "Tanis, take the guard, escort Trelanth and her party."

He saluted and led the way into the trees with Trelanth at his side and the others close behind.

The road was completely empty of traffic, nothing moved. Like a silent tide the Elves poured out of the forest and onto that poorly paved surface. The wagon Tanis had abandoned was brought back into service to carry three injured and a half dozen or more younger children.

Every Elf with a horse carried a passenger, either child or elder. The queen rode her mighty charger up and down the long line of Elves with a crippled boy clinging to her waist, for some reason he had not gone through to Sanctuary with the others. As she stopped on a small rise to watch she heard a soft voice behind her.

"Queen Ariel?"

She tilted her head back a bit to hear him better. "Yes?"

"You should kill me now, and throw the body into the trees."

"Why would I do a thing like that?"

"I'm crippled, Lady. I'm useless, and I'll endanger the others by holding them back. I thought I could keep up, but now I see that's not true."

"Who said this to you?"

"No one, Lady, it was my own thought."

Ariel patted the hands around her waist gently. "Then you need a new thought. What's your name?"

"I have none, Lady."

"I see. Have you learned the old stories of our people?"

"Some, Lady."

"Do you know the tale of Kern, the lame horseman?"

"I do. He was lame on the ground, but with his horse he was a mighty warrior."

"That's right, what else?"

"He became the Great Queen's horseman, the man who tended and trained her horses."

"Indeed so, that's the tale of it. Now, young sir, Grimm seems to like you. I name you, Kern. It is now your task to learn as much as you can about horses. It is said Kern of old could talk to them and they to him. I command you now to learn as much as you can of horses, and if you do well, you will become the keeper of my horses. Will you take on this task for me?"

"Oh, my queen, I swear I'll do everything in my power to learn," he enthused.

"Elves and horses work well together, Kern. I knew nothing of horses, but I was alone and sick, and someone had left a horse for me. I spoke to her and begged her to take me to the others in my party. This she did willingly. Never show anger or abuse to a horse, and they will serve you well. Remember."

"I will, my queen, I promise."

"Then come, Kern, we must find you a horse of your own. Until then you will ride with me and tend to Grimm for me." With a laugh of joy, she touched her heels lightly to the big war horse's flanks and he surged ahead. She brought him to an easy canter and headed to the other side of the road.

Ariel smiled and turned aside for a swift ride through the open fields and back again, she'd felt the arms around her waist tighten and the shudder as the boy sobbed in relief. He would not be killed as useless, as his master had threatened to do. He would have a life, a task, and a name given by the queen herself. When she felt he was ready, she turned the big horse back to the head of the column.

When darkness forced them to stop and make camp, she showed Kern how to take off the saddle and rub down the horse. She smiled with delight as he talked softly to the massive beast. When Ariel turned back Mearith and Arlon were grinning at her. "What?"

"It seems you have a new groomsman, my delight."

"I have. This man is Kern. Kern will ride with me until we can find him a horse of his own."

Tanis grinned and winked at the boy. "My Lady, we acquired several horses just yesterday. There was a likely looking mare in the bunch. She looks like she'd be happier with a rider instead of carrying a pack."

"Was there a saddle, Tanis?"

"Yes, Lady. We brought it in the wagon. Shall I ...?"

Ariel grinned. "Why are you still here?"

With a laugh, he was up and away. A short time later he returned leading a lively young mare who fairly pranced along beside him. He passed the reins to Kern then began to show him how to care for the horse.

"It was just one year ago, Lady Mearith was teaching me these things. We all have much to learn, but you're the lucky one. You'll get to spend every day with horses."

Ariel was smiling at them. "Ariel?"

"He wanted me to kill him, Mearith. He thought himself a liability, that he would slow us all down and put us in danger because of his lame leg."

"So you named him Kern and gave him a horse."

"I did, yes. Do you disapprove?"

"Oh no, my delight, never that. Once again you rise above all expectation."

For that night and the next two, the chain of fire glowed along the roadside of the Shotar Highway. Scouts ranged well ahead and guards watched closely from behind, but they traveled the road for three full days and encountered no one.

By the end of the third day messages were being sent from the front of the column to the rear and it was Kern on his horse who carried them. Tanis had been right; the young mare was the right choice for the boy.

None of them could have known she was bred for racing, and had been on her way to the new governor of Magdan as a gift. The boy and the horse bonded instantly and, as all true Elves, he had a natural affinity for horses.

Ariel was astride Grimm, trotting alongside the column when he approached at a gallop. He didn't dismount and kneel as she'd forbidden it because of his lame leg. Kneeling was painful for him. "Ho, Kern, what news of the front?"

"They've arrived unhindered, my queen. Already they enter the forest again. Lady, there is an Orc waiting there to speak with you."

"Drakkat is there?"

"Yes, Lady, that was the name."

"Then let's go." She urged Grimm into a gallop, but Kern raced ahead to let them know she was coming. She arrived to find Drakkat waiting with Mearith and Arlon.

"Drakkat," she shouted, as she leaped from her horse and hugged him. "What brings you here, dear friend?"

The big Orc just grinned. "I bring the supplies as ordered by that arrogant Elf, Evanseth. He dumped the lot in my lap and ordered me to bring it to you, then walked away. It took every horse we had plus what we could borrow from Marc just to get it here."

"That is welcome news. What have you brought me?"

"Cloaks, boots, tunics, leggings, and the like, plus a healer."

"A healer?"

"It is I, Lady Ariel," smiled a young Elf, as she approached and knelt.

"Beren, rise and embrace me. You've decided to travel with us?"

"Yes, Lady," replied the girl, as she released the queen and stepped back. "I've learned much from Meg, and much more from Egma."

"I thought age had robbed Egma of her wits?"

Beren laughed. "Lady, Egma believed me to be her youngest daughter, and she tried to teach me as much of the healing arts as she could. She has more to teach, I'm sure, but I felt the people on this journey would need me more as Meg will remain with Marc in Fugitive."

"It was well reasoned out, Beren, and I'm thrilled you're here. We do have great need of your skills. Back along the trail there is a wagon with folk who would surely benefit from your attentions."

"Then, with your permission, Lady, I'll be about the task." She gathered up her bag of supplies and stepped away, but Ariel's voice stopped her.

"Beren wait, Kern can get you there far more swiftly." The boy moved the horse closer. Drakkat grabbed the girl and tossed her up behind the rider.

"Hang on tight," said Kern. As soon as her arms gripped him he wheeled the horse and sped away, Beren's sudden shriek lingering on the air.

"Boy's reckless," said Drakkat. "I like that. So, what'll I do with all this gear that's wearing down my horses?"

"Arlon, have someone take inventory and distribute what Drakkat's brought us to the most needy."

It was long past dark when the last of the Elves were safely in the forest and settled down by a campfire. "All right, Drakkat, what else is on your mind?" asked Ariel.

"Hmm," muttered the big Orc, a smile coming to his lips. "We've had word from the mountains, Lady. The news isn't good. A small band of Dwarves found their way into Fugitive a few days past. They bring tales of strange things, and of Geni disturbing the lands near the Ruins of Elanda. What they searched for, the Dwarves did not know."

"I can guess," muttered Trelanth. "They know what's happened and they fear reprisals for past deeds. Ever the unworthy see retribution looming and seek to forestall it."

Drakkat chuckled at that. "It's true, the Geni have no honor, and what you say is most likely."

"But?"

"But this camp holds an untold wealth of slaves. Our queen has impoverished many, including many of the Geni."

"I care not for their motives," sighed Ariel. "At this point I would prefer to avoid them if possible. Mearith, your thoughts on this?"

"It will add many days to our journey, but there is a way, another path we could take. It will lead us to a hidden valley deep in the mountains. There's a river and forest there, and if desperate we could winter there safely.

"The place would be vulnerable as a permanent home, but as a waystation it'll serve well enough."

"Could we establish a permanent waystation there?"

"We could. What's on your mind, my delight?"

"If the weather turns against us there are many among us who could benefit from resting there for the winter. Would this be possible?"

"Yes. Are you suggesting we take them there?"

"Only if we must, but in future I would like to establish several waystations between Elfhome and Fugitive. These stations would be manned by Elves well skilled in woodcraft, easily able to foresee the advance of enemies and avoid them as well as warn all Elves of the danger.

"Ah well, thoughts for another time. For now, we need a way to get our people to Elfhome safely."

"There is something else you might consider, Lady Ariel," said Drakkat.

"And that is?"

"The Geni have sent most of their forces south, thinking you went that way. Strike them hard while their guard is down."

"Explain."

"You're pressed for time. A few mages and treasure seekers are poking about in your path. Strike hard and fast, destroy them, and pass through. You'll be long gone before the Geni can recall their forces. Yes, they will watch that road carefully in future. That's the time to establish the way points."

"My people are weak, Drakkat, and the warriors with us are dedicated to protecting them. I would not risk my people so soon, besides, if the mages are disturbing the old magics, ..."

"Actually, I believe Drakkat's right, my delight. Do not fear the mages, for I now believe these are not the mighty magic users of old. What think you, Trelanth?"

"I think I'd like to see what these mages are about, poking through the Ruins of Elanda."

"When we passed that way with Evenseth earlier this year I was disturbed by that place," said Ariel.

"In what way, dear heart?"

"It called to me, Mearith, my heart. I heard it whisper my name, call to me to return, to embrace what once was, to rise again as before, Queen of the High Born. I felt the stone that rides at my breast respond to it."

"Another test?"

"Yes, and not one I want to face with so many newly freed to care for. Perhaps you and I, with Trelanth and the guard, I might, but with so many ..."

"My queen, if I may."

"Speak, Arlon, advise me in this."

"Lady, you told me to focus on getting the people to Elfhome as quickly as possible. Each day we lose on this journey is precious, for the year grows late, especially in Elfhome. The world is colder there, as it will be in the mountains. I believe Drakkat has the right of it."

Ariel sat quietly for several moments, staring into the fire. No one disturbed her thoughts. At length, she sighed and squared her shoulders. "Trelanth, are you aware of any prying eyes upon us?"

"There are none, Lady Ariel."

"Prepare then. When the sun rises, the people will begin moving toward the Ruins of Elanda. Mearith and I will ride ahead with fifty warriors chosen by Arlon, Tanis and the guard will accompany us as well."

"And me too?" asked Trelanth.

"Yes, you and your mages. Our people will be safe enough, for we'll be the focus of all attention, if there is any."

"Perhaps there may not be, Lady."

"Trelanth?"

"Ethor is excellent at masking spells. He may be able to hide our activities from all within the city of Shotar. Only those we encounter might be aware of us."

"Excellent. That would truly please me."

"I'll meet you on the road, my delight. I think I should have a look at this path first hand before we go charging in."

Ariel just nodded as Mearith rose and trotted into the forest. "Drakkat, of all the people here to advise me, you've traveled the most in the world as it is now. Have you ever been to Shotar?"

"I've been in that city many times, my queen."

"We estimate they sent over a thousand men south to catch us. How many more warriors might they have in the city?"

A wide grin spread across his face and he chuckled. "Enough to defend it, perhaps, but not many more."

"Drakkat, old friend, from a warrior's perspective, what's the overall state of affairs in the world?"

"In the world? Well, from what I've seen over the years, this part of the world is ruled by the Geni. They rule by threat of force and magic. They keep the only standing army of professional soldiers, mostly humans and orcs. This army is spread out through the five cities."

"Like Magdan."

"Yes, Magdan is one of them."

"How many men do you think this army of theirs has?"

Drakkat was silent as he thought about that. "Perhaps fifteen thousand soldiers plus slaves and supply handlers. Most of them are stationed in the two cities to the south and west. The one guards against the raiders from the sea, and the other from the creatures of the south."

"Tell me of the sea raiders."

"I know nothing of them, Lady. I've seen their ships, but that's all. They seem to be both Orc and human, perhaps deserters from the ancient wars were their ancestors."

"And the southern threat?"

"All I know is what I've heard in the streets and taverns. Wandering tribes of Geni who were left behind when the Geni led their forces north so long ago. There are also Ogres, Giants, and other creatures that evolved from the ages of Geni magics, twisted, evil things, fit only for killing."

"Their numbers?"

"Unknown, Lady Ariel, but not so many that they would dare come north in force."

"Hmmm, Arlon, you were here when the world was broken, yes?"

"I was, my queen."

"Tell me of that time, the numbers of peoples."

"Lady, in those days the numbers of Elves, both Borni and High Born, were as the trees in the forest, many thousands beyond count. The Humans were few at that time, but the Dwarves were many as well.

"First the free Orc clans came from the south, driven from behind by the Geni forces. Drakkat's clan was one such. They tried to forge a new home for themselves, and allied themselves with the Humans.

"Once that alliance started to carve out a territory from the forest, we took notice and began to push them back south, but the Geni forces came then, hundreds of thousands of them and more, as there were of us.

"The great war ravaged the lands and diminished their number as well as our own, but they kept coming. The land was different then, but in the end, it was broken by the Geni. The magic of the High Born was too strong for them, and so they broke the world to release the demons."

"What happened then?"

"The High Born twisted the cataclysm so it consumed all. As the vast forests sank into the sea, swallowing most of the armies as well as the demons, the Borni left this realm."

"Arlon, speak to me of the numbers, the numbers of peoples now as compared to then."

"From what I've seen since returning, Lady, it's a sad thing. We Elves are so few compared to what we were, but the Geni seemed to have fared worse. It's my guess the High Born gamble was successful in destroying the armies of demons and invaders, but in so doing they exhausted themselves and were vulnerable.

"The Humans seem to have grown greatly in numbers and the Orcs appear to be recovering. The Dwarves fared much worse as their mountains took most of them beneath the seas when they sank."

"So, from what you tell me, am I to understand that, compared to the world before the Breaking, this land is somewhat uninhabited?"

"Yes, Lady, the great cities of yore are gone. Those that have arisen are but villages in comparison to what was."

"What are you thinking, Lady Ariel?" asked Drakkat.

"If I understand this correctly, it wasn't just the Elves who were decimated by the War of Breaking. With the addition of the Borni, perhaps the Elves are as numerous as the rest in comparison. If this is true, what would be the Geni's natural reaction, if they did discover us in the forest so near the city?"

Everyone close looked up at Drakkat's great bellow of laughter. "Those sniveling cowards would hide in their city, bracing the gates against a possible attack from the Elves.

"If there is an attack from them at all, it will come from magic."

"My thought as well, old friend. Trelanth, what say you?"

"The reasoning is sound, my queen. I will prepare the mages; we'll be ready for whatever they try."

"Prepare then, my friend, for tomorrow we march. Three days from now promises to be an interesting day."

The Ruins of Elanda

The journey that would take Ariel and her troops two days, Mearith accomplished in a day. She didn't bother to leave markers for Ariel to follow, the Pull would lead her in the right direction.

Mearith pushed her horse hard until they reached the edge of the forest near the mountain path. She dismounted and stripped off the saddle then rubbed the tired animal down. Crooning softly to the beast as she worked, she reapplied the saddle then hung the bridle on the pommel, and sent him back to Ariel. As the horse softly nuzzled her then trotted away she smiled.

The trail led upwards into the mountains, then out onto a broad plateau. As she ran, she remembered how the city had shone in the sunlight, a true work of wonder. That plateau had been a forested valley in those long past days. Now, Elanda lay in ruins on a cold wind-swept mountainside.

The day was growing dark as Mearith approached her target. She could see two campfires, close together. As silently as a ghost the Elvish assassin moved in closer.

She felt the sudden tingle of ethereal energy as she tripped the mage's wards. Grinning with mischief she gave the snorting grunt of a startled boar and tossed a stone across the campsite.

There was a crackle of energy then a small fireball exploded where her thrown stone had landed. "Another of those thrice damned pig things," grumbled a voice. "Did you get him, Mage? Are we having pork for supper tonight?"

"Shut up or I'll turn you into a frog. Those damned things would make a meal off you if I didn't keep them at bay. Speaking of supper, one of you will have to go hunting in the morning. We're out of meat again."

The men continued to grumble and Mearith slipped away to the next campfire. She was more careful this time and was able to sense the wards. The first had been human cast, but these were Geni, far more familiar.

During the War of World Breaking, Mearith had slipped past many such wards. The memories returned easily as she softly breathed the chant that allowed her to pass through undetected. This camp contained three Geni and an Elf slave.

Fierce blue eyes watch as the young Elf served the meal and accepted the abuse of her masters. "Be careful, you nearly slopped that on me. I swear, if you burn me I'll withhold the oshar and watch you die slowly of madness."

"Relax, it's not the slave's fault we can't find the library."

"She's a descendant of the High Born, she should be drawn to it instinctively."

"Those instincts were lost to the slaves long ago, I'm sure. We probably bred that out of them ourselves. No, we'll have to do this the hard way."

"What I don't understand," said the third, and much older Geni, "is why we can't detect it ourselves. It was obviously hidden magically, we should be able to detect the residue of that spell."

"Yes, well, there's nothing but spell residue in this accursed place. I'm sure we can detect it, but try to identify it, there's the trick."

"If it was easy it would have been found long ago and another would wield the power it contains. We must be patient, we will find it, and when we do we'll bring that upstart King to his knees.

"When I was a child the king would shake in fear each time a true mage walked by. We will find the library of the High Born Queen, and we'll gain the secrets of their power. When that day comes, there'll be a new king in Shotar."

"Speaking of which, what should we do about the new Queen of the High Born. What if she comes for her library?"

"She went south, to the wide forests there," replied the elder Geni. "We watched her go ourselves. No, we have a chance, but time is growing short. We have to find it before the snows fall."

"What about the human?"

"Which one?"

"The mage. Do we share the knowledge with him? I don't like the idea of a human being able to wield that kind of power."

"Fear not, my young friend. The captain of the guardsmen has his orders. The instant we have the prize in sight he'll put a sword through that would-be mage."

"Good idea. Ah, just think of it, to be able to wield the power as they did in the War of Conquest, to actually have the power to call forth a demon."

"A demon? They called legions of them, then that accursed Elf Queen broke the world and flooded the lands, killing every living thing."

"It was well she did," sighed the elder mage, "for had she not the world would be ruled by demons. I haven't told you this, but I found the hidden passages in Merkon's diaries. There was no secret spell of power there, just the tale of it.

"Yes, our forbearers called forth the demons, but they realized too late their mistake. At the moment the Elf Queen struck, they dropped their protections from the demon armies. Instead they focused on protecting the Geni.

"Because of this, we survived and the Elves fell. Had they continued to protect the demon legions they would have overrun the world. As it was, the few who remained were sent back to their own realm, but the power of that spell burned away the last of the great mages' abilities. We have continued to decline ever since that time.

"The humans grow steadily in numbers, their mages grow in power, the Orcs and Dwarves are increasing in numbers again, and that's not the worst of it. Things like those boar men, the swamp giants, and many more are growing stronger as the Geni continue to decline. We need the knowledge and power contained in that library. With it we can restore the Geni."

"And rule them all," said the youngest.

"Yes," agreed the elder, "and rule them all. That's why we're out here on this forsaken mountain side, freezing our buttocks off."

Mearith had heard enough. Silent as a shadow she withdrew and returned to the shelter of the jumbled boulders and scrub trees at the edge of the ruins. At dawn, she set out to meet Ariel.

ARIEL AND HER TROOPS met Mearith's war horse just inside the tree line. She dismounted and approached. The big horse nuzzled her affectionately. "So, she left you behind, was that out of necessity or a desire for stealth. I'm betting on stealth.

"Kern, it's as I suspected. Wait here and tend the horses until Arlon catches up. Things should be well in hand by then. Let's go, people." Slinging her bow across her back she led them up the rocky trail. Night was falling when she sensed Mearith's nearness.

Smiling brightly, she stood in the trail and opened her arms. Chuckling with delight, Mearith stepped from behind a boulder and embraced her. "We should camp here until near dawn, no fires for they are close. Gather round and I'll tell you what I've learned."

"So, our guess was right, Trelanth," said Ariel, as Mearith finished her tale. "These are not the mighty Geni mages of old."

"It appears so, Lady. This is both good and bad. My queen, the Geni must never be allowed to find that library."

"I agree, Trelanth. However, it's remained hidden for centuries, we must hope it remains that way a little longer. First, we dispose of these Geni and their guards, then we get our people to Elfhome. Once there, we'll discuss what's to be done about the library."

"If we can even find it."

"Oh, I can find it, I'm sure, but first we need a key to open it."

"A key, Lady?"

"Yes, and Mearith knows where it is, or, at least where it was."

Mearith's eyes opened wide. "The cave."

Ariel nodded and patted the stone that hung around her neck. "So my friend tells me."

The stone was glowing, throbbing with a life of its own. Mearith saw and gave Ariel a questioning look. She shrugged and tucked it back inside her tunic. "Behave," she whispered, as she patted the stone.

They were awakened by Mearith near dawn. They rose and she led them toward the camps of the searchers. Silently they approached then settled into hiding, weapons drawn. Trelanth whispered to Ariel who nodded then whispered to Mearith.

She obviously didn't like it, but she nodded then turned and spoke softly to the warrior next to her. Like the whispers of a winter's breeze, the message spread through the war band of Elves.

As the day dawned, and the sun arose, the camps began to stir. The guards were still rubbing sleep from their eyes when Trelanth strode into their midst. "What seek you here, trespassers?"

She was instantly hit with bolts of energy from different directions. She staggered back, but didn't fall. With a laugh and a spoken word, she brushed aside the next attack. Her shield was glowing and crackling with energy.

Ariel signaled with her hand and, with a sound like sighing wind, thirty bows released their arrows. The entire group, including the mages, fell. The elder Geni mage tried to pull the arrow from his side. "How? How is this possible?"

"From the bow of the High Born Queen was your fate delivered, Geni," said a terrible voice behind him.

He turned to see her standing there, bow in hand and shining with energy, as he sank to his knees. She was glowing with the power that coursed through her. "Did you think to steal what is mine from the glory your ancestors destroyed?"

She squatted down beside him where he lay dying. "Know this, I will free my people from the chains of slavery, and then I will drive the rest of your kin before me. I will destroy you all or push you back to the barren lifeless lands from whence you came."

She rose with a liquid grace and stepped away. "Finish them. Loot, then hide, the bodies. We'll remain here until all have passed safely beyond."

As the Elves worked Ariel saw the look of deep concern on Mearith's face. She stepped closer and reached for her lover. "What troubles you, my heart?"

"Who speaks through your lips, my delight? Is it you who speaks through the stone, or the stone who speaks through you?"

Ariel sighed and melted into Mearith's arms. "It's neither, dear heart, but the spirit of she who fell here. I heard her whisper to me, and I granted her this much. The stone focused her energy and she spoke through me. She's at peace now and has blessed our quest."

"Truly, this is so?"

"Yes, love. The stone hasn't claimed me, nor has the spirit of she who made it. All is well. We will remain here to make certain our people pass through unhindered then we'll rejoin them.

"Mearith, that library holds far more than a few books of magic, it holds the literature and all knowledge of my people. It contains the very soul of who they were."

"You want to find and reclaim it."

"I do, yes, not just to keep it out of the hands of the Geni, but to allow our people a chance to learn of who they came from. I won't deviate from the path I've chosen for the Bornani, but I still think they should know the truth."

"I agree, my delight, but this isn't the time."

"No, it isn't. We have much to do before we try to reclaim that library."

"Should we leave people here to make certain the Geni don't stumble on it by accident?"

"They won't, for it isn't here. It was all she would be able to preserve of her people, so she trans-located it before she cast the Spell of Breaking."

"She told you where it is?" Ariel grinned and nodded. "Are you going to tell me?" Ariel whispered softly in her ear. "Are you joking? Narthwood? That's where it is?"

Ariel nodded. "Not a word."

"My lips are sealed," grinned Mearith.

THEY WOULD HAVE TWO full days to wait for Arlon to arrive and yet another for the marchers to pass. While they waited, Ariel wandered about the area, exploring some of the partially fallen buildings, wandering some of the ruined streets.

Mearith kept her company, staying back to allow her time to absorb all she saw. She suspected Ariel was communing with the jewel and the spirit of her ancestor.

At one point Ariel turned to face Mearith, but Mearith knew it wasn't Ariel. "Release her. Release her or I'll carry her far from this place, never to return."

"This you will do anyway, Borni Princess. Be at peace, daughter of the forest, I'm not the enemy here, she freely allows me this. Recall the day we argued, you and I."

"I remember, Queen Onlay. You should have come with us."

"No, Princess, I could not, you know this. Had we done so, the Elves would fade from the realms forever. On that day, I saw what would happen, and I knew you were the only hope, that it would be you, Princess, who would pull the thread to unravel all the Geni had wrought.

"I did what I had to do to ensure the Elves' survival. Guard her well, Princess of the Borni, treasure her. In time, you may come to fear her, but know this, Queen Ariel will ever be yours. If she gets lost, you need only remind her of the bond you share."

"What are you going to do?"

"Remember what I've said."

As the voice of the spirit stopped speaking, Ariel screamed as powerful energies crackled around her, flinging Mearith back. She screamed again, but this time it was as much a wild laugh of victory as a scream. The energies suddenly withdrew into her and Ariel sank to the ground moaning.

As the others came running, Mearith gathered Ariel into her arms. She felt the surge as strength returned to her lover and Ariel rose easily to her feet. "Ariel?"

"I'm all right, my heart, my friends. Before we return to camp for a meal, there is something I must do. Trelanth, make certain what I do goes unobserved."

"Of course, my queen."

Ariel squeezed Mearith's arm and gave her a gentle smile. "I will reveal all as soon as I've finished this one small task."

She trotted away until she reached the crumbled remains of a tower. With a wave of her hand the rubble was cast aside, spraying broken stone in many directions. There, before Ariel, lay the remains of a body in royal garb.

At a signal from Ariel's hand the bones rose into the air and floated away. Ariel followed until the body came to rest. Another wave of her hand thrust aside more rubble exposing a staircase going down. "Come, Mearith, Trelanth, we will lay Queen Onlay to rest with her ancestors.

The body floated down the stairs and they followed. At their passage the walls began to glow, shedding enough light for them to see clearly. They reached the bottom to see row upon row of stone coffins, each with the carved image of its owner on top.

As the body approached one, the lid slid aside and it entered. The lid slid closed and Ariel laid her hand gently on the cold stone. "Rest now, Great Grandmother, the task is mine now. You've prepared me well, and now you must rest.

"As I promised you, the High Born will be re-born as the Bornani, but the library will be found, the histories revealed. You will be remembered, not as the mad queen who broke the world, but as the woman who sacrificed all so Elfkind could continue to survive, to grow strong again. Be at peace."

Ariel, followed closely by Mearith and Trelanth, returned to the surface. Once outside she turned and spoke a single word. The rubble she had cast aside to reveal the crypt returned to its former position. The final resting place of Queen Onlay was well hidden.

Ariel nodded her satisfaction then turned away. "Come, let's get back to camp. I'm hungry as a bear in springtime."

There was meat cooking as they reached the camp and Ariel set to with a will. When she finished eating her fill, she sighed with delight and leaned her back against Mearith's shoulder.

"My people, I have a tale to tell. I know you saw much of what happened here today. I will explain, reveal the rest.

"When we arrived here yesterday, I encountered the spirit of my ancestor, she who fought that final battle. The Geni teach that it was she who broke the world."

"Another lie?" asked Tanis.

"Yes, another lie. The Geni cracked the world open and released a horde of demons onto the battlefield, but they lost control of them. Some of you were here when that happened.

"Queen Onlay had been in her tower, and she saw the death of all Elves everywhere. She saw the sterility and stagnation of the Borni in Sanctuary, and she saw the death of all Elves who remained behind.

"There was only one chance and she took it. As soon as the Borni were away she cast the spell of breaking and turned it back against the demon hordes. Her spell was more powerful than that of the Geni, for she held nothing back. Yes, she deliberately released all her life force and broke the world as we know it.

"As she hoped, the forces of the enemy were so devastated they could not finish the destruction they'd begun, and so the Elves survived. Her two daughters survived, but with no memories.

"All who remained aware on the battlefield were the Orcs and humans. It was many days later the Geni regained their senses, and by then the Elves were in slave chains and our path was set.

"Queen Onlay sacrificed herself, her children, her people, to ensure Elfkind would survive. She sacrificed all to give the Borni time to escape because she knew you would be needed one day, be the key to Elvish survival. At the end, she knew we all needed to reunite and return to the forest, there to be nurtured back to health as a people.

"This day she gave the last of her strength to me and released her spirit which she had bound to this place. This day we laid her to rest with her kin, the last of the true High Born."

"Lady Ariel, I have studied magic all my life, and am considered one of the strongest, but I felt in you a power well beyond my reach. I feel it even now."

"Be at peace, Trelanth. I'm queen of the Bornani. This day we laid the last of the High Born to her final bed. She told me that it was our use of the High Power that first caught the attention of the Geni.

"Until the High Born reached into that universal well of creation, this world was unknown to the Geni. Their own world was dying and so they sought another. It was the lure of unlimited power that drew them here.

"We will not revisit that, but will embrace the magics of the forest, of life. The things we build we will build with our hands, not the power of magic. However, with magic we will help the forest grow, heal hurts and wounds, bring warm rains and nurturing sunny days, soft snows in winter. These are the magics I want for my people."

Everyone had relaxed again. Trelanth smiled. "I like that vision, Lady, but what of the library they sought? If the Geni should find it ..."

"They will not," grinned Ariel, "for I know where it is, she showed it to me. The Geni will not find it, Trelanth, but one day we will explore it together, then return it to the Elves so all may learn the history, art, and beauty of our people, who they were, what their lives were like, and more.

"The High Born are no more, nor will they ever return, but they contributed much to this world, saved it from complete destruction, and I would have them remembered. When we pass from this place, much that is within me now may remain behind. Rest now, my friends, for Arlon will arrive with the sun tomorrow."

Guards were posted, then the rest settled down for the night. Ariel cuddled into Mearith's arms and sighed. Mearith kissed her hair and cuddled her closer. "Rest now, my delight. You've had an eventful day."

"You know, don't you?"

"That the power will always be with you now? Oh yes, I know. So does Trelanth."

"Mearith, my heart, it frightens me. What will I become?"

"Whatever you wish to be, my treasure."

"So, this is another test? The power is another tool, a weapon to use or not as I choose? I can use or refuse it by force of will?"

"Exactly so, my sweet. That was the lesson she tried to teach, what she tried to express to me that day so long ago, when she refused to send her people with the Borni. She had held herself in check as long as she could, but in the end, she did what she had to do, and paid the price for it."

"The price?"

"For thousands of years her spirit has lingered here, lingered in the clear knowledge she had sacrificed her people to an uncertain future, the knowledge that she had destroyed the world as she knew it, the agony of what she had done, and powerless to influence the events that followed.

"Well, perhaps not quite powerless, but more helpless. Only today, at the last, do I understand what she tried to tell me so long ago. Only now do I understand what she meant when she told me to run, to save myself and my people for the future."

"Mearith?"

"I came to the tower with the last of the Borni warriors. We had sent the rest of our people through the portals, but we were ready to stand at her side. She told me to get out, to remain free at all cost, then she shut us out from the battlefield.

"We could see her people being slaughtered and felt the world tremble at her call, and we fled. To our undying shame, we fled. She tried to shield our retreat, but a single arrow pierced that shield."

"The arrow that took your lover."

"Yes, that one. I wonder now if that one was let through with a purpose, how much of the future she actually saw. No matter. Onlay did what she had to do, as will we. That time is long past, and we shall let it rest with her. Now we must build the future she sacrificed herself for."

"So you're not angry with me, or afraid of me?"

"No, my delight, whatever makes you think I might be angry or frightened?"

"Because it might look like I had forsaken the quest, embraced the seductive power of the High Magic."

"No, my sweet, I'm not angry or afraid. I know you, your heart, your devotion to the quest, to your people. You have access to incredible power now, and that can be seductive, but she gave me the key to bringing you back."

"She did? What is it ...?" Ariel got no further as Mearith kissed her lips, putting all the love she had into it, channeling the power of the Pull as much as she could.

Ariel moaned softly and melted completely into her arms. "Oh, by all the gods, yes, that'll do it every time. There's no greater magic than your kiss, no stronger force than the Pull."

"Settle down in my arms, my delight. The people will arrive tomorrow, and we must protect their passage." Ariel fairly purred as she drifted off to sleep.

In her dreams, Ariel climbed to the top of a high tower and there she saw Queen Onlay waiting for her. Onlay took Ariel's hand and led her to the wall where they could look out over the city of the High Born. Ariel smiled in wonder at the shining city and its beautiful people below.

Slowly the scene shifted as the armies of the Geni arrived. She saw the cracking of the world and watched sorrowfully as the great city turned to rubble, the lands heave and change as the seas swept the combatants from the field. The city faded into mist and vast forests grew.

Ariel saw movement in those forests. The scene moved closer, and she could see Elf children chasing each other through the glades, homes being grown from living trees, hear voices raised in song, songs so beautiful they brought tears to her eyes.

The forest gave way to fields and farms, and then to towns where Elves, Men, Orcs, Dwarves, and more, traded and worked together in harmony and to common benefit.

The scene drew back until Ariel was standing on the tower with her ancestor once again. "That is the dream, my daughter out of time, that's the vision I held for you to claim. I've given you the power to make it become reality. The road is long, and fraught with danger, but I trust in the purity of your heart, the force of your determination, and the love of our people that we both share.

"That devotion to the people was ever the hallmark of the royal line, Ariel. Go now, my daughter across time, go create the dream for me, for us, for the people."

"For the people," Ariel said, still deep in sleep.

"Yes, my delight, for the people," smiled Mearith, as she, too, allowed sleep to claim her.

Found

Nine Elves sat beside a small fire, huddled together for warmth. The two cloaks donated by the warriors, L'ark and his brother L'mak, were spread over them as well as possible. The chill of the heavy mist didn't help.

Most of them had already passed through the awakening, but not all. Tereen, L'ark's mate, did her best to comfort them, but she had only recently passed through that mystery herself. She hoped and prayed L'ark would soon return, and she dared not hope he would have Telee with him.

They had been methodically searching every farm they came to. They rescued slaves where they could, but it was dangerous, and somehow the word had spread, Elves were stealing the slaves. The farmers were hiding their slaves as well as guarding them with dogs and weapons.

While Tereen talked softly and tried to sooth the more recently freed woman, L'ark grinned as he approached the farmhouse. They could hear the wild barking of the hounds. "You think this is funny," groused L'mak."

"Hey, it's your turn, what can I say? Get ready, I hear the door opening." The door was flung wide and with the farmer roaring for them to "get the bastards," the hounds charged from the house.

L'mak was up and away, making sure the hounds saw him. He ran straight for the forest away from their small camp. As swift and agile as an Elf warrior is, a hound is faster. L'mak barely made it into the tree's welcoming branches before the three huge hounds reached him.

Still grinning, L'ark slid easily in behind the farmer who was standing in the yard now, shouting encouragements to the dogs. A blade appeared at the man's throat and a soft voice sounded in his ear. "Relax and be still, my friend. Good. Now, here we go, inside, easy now."

L'ark marched the man back inside then pushed him toward his frightened family. "We don't have any slaves, so you're wasting your time, Elf."

L'ark passed the dagger from his right hand to his left and slid the sword from its scabbard. "I've been watching this farm for days. Bring out your slaves or I'll kill you all and find them myself."

As he spoke the woman whimpered and pulled her two smallest children closer to her. "Do as he says, he means it. Think of the children, Jord, give him the damned slaves."

"We'll be ruined, they'll take the farm."

"We'll still be alive. For pity's sake, think of the children. Do as he says."

Defeated, the man took a key from the cord around his neck and passed it to a boy of about fifteen. "Boy, I can see it in your eyes," said L'ark. "Don't try it. I've been a warrior since before the world was broken. If you truly want to be the hero, do as you're told, keep your family alive."

Glaring his hate at the invader, the boy continued to the side of the house and pulled up a carpet, exposing a huge lock. He inserted the key and twisted. The lock fell open and he tossed it aside then lifted the trap door. "Come up," he said harshly.

Five slaves crawled up the shaky ladder and stood gazing at L'ark, terrified. "Is that everybody?" he asked. One of the slaves nodded. "All right then, come outside. I'll take you away from here. No one will ever whip you again."

He stepped aside and let them pass. "Now, good people, I caution you not to follow us, death awaits you on that path." He tossed a small bag to the woman who, startled, nearly missed catching it. It was a bag of money, more than she had ever seen in her life.

"Use that money to buy beasts to help with the farm. If I come back here and find you've bought more slaves, I'll kill the lot of you." With that, he stepped outside to see L'mak leading the slaves away and the three hounds chewing contentedly on the bones of the deer L'mak had fed them. He hurried to catch up.

"You're being followed," said L'mak.

"Damn kid," muttered L'ark. "Be right back." He slipped away into the mist, but returned a few moments later.

"You kill him?"

"No, but it'll take him a while to get himself untied then he'll have to go home for more clothes. Maybe this time he'll learn. So, people, my name is L'ark and this lad is my brother, L'mak. We'll take you to a safe place where you can live in peace, but I'll explain all that later. Right now, I'm looking for someone special. Is Telee among you?"

The poor woman stumbled and nearly fell. L'mak reached out to take her arm and steady her. "That was my name when I was young," she replied hesitantly.

L'ark was instantly at her side. "Does the name Tereen have meaning for you?"

"That was my mother's name."

"And Ariel?"

A faint smile touched her lips. "A friend from long ago. Why do you ask me these things? What do you know of these people?"

"I will reunite you with them," he replied, as they reached the wider part of the trail. "Ariel is now queen of all Elfkind, and she sent me to find you. Come, Tereen is near."

Another bend in the trail revealed the small camp and a waiting Tereen. She flew into L'ark's arms. "Thank the gods you're all right. Did you ..." She stopped speaking as she saw Telee in the group.

"Mother, is that truly you?"

"Telee, oh my darling girl," sobbed Tereen, as she hugged her daughter tightly. "I feared to never see you alive again."

"You nearly didn't. Oh mother, I have missed you so. Those people did unspeakable things to me, to us all."

"Never again, my darling girl, never again. You're free now and we'll take you deep into the forests. There you will learn to be a true Elf again, even as I am learning."

"How did you get here? How did you ever find me?"

"Sit here by the fire with me, Telee. I'll tell you how I came to be here, and of your childhood friend who didn't forget you, nor the promise you made to each other."

"You mean Ariel? You've seen her? She remembers how we promised to free each other?"

Tereen smiled through her tears and hugged Telee again. "Yes, I've seen Ariel. Telee, Ariel is the Queen of the High Born Elves returned. She's broken free, recalled the Borni from the mists of time, and she is freeing all the slaves. When she saw me in the numbers she brought out of Magdan, she sent L'ark and I to find you."

"L'ark?"

"It was the compulsion, Telee. I went to the well for water, and I felt it. I was terrified, but I felt him getting closer and couldn't move, I was rooted to the spot. He came to me, threw a cloak about my shoulders, then took me away while his friends started a fight to distract the Watch from our escape.

"I didn't know it, but Magdan was full to bursting with Borni, with Ariel leading them. It was the time of the great auction. They defeated the Geni and took all the slaves into the forest. When she saw me she asked about you, and then sent us to find you."

Suddenly great wracking sobs shook the girl's body as her mother held her again. "She remembered. Ariel remembered. So many times I tried to escape into the forest. Death by madness would be so much better than the life I've had, but they always caught me and took me back. The punishments were horrible.

"Are you going to take me to Ariel before the madness takes me?"

"No girl," said L'ark, "the year is growing late, and the journey is hard. We have a number of you now and no supplies to face that track through the mountains in winter. No, we will head for Fugitive."

"The master said that place doesn't exist. Every time he punished me he asked where I thought I was going. I had to tell him to stop the pain. I always said Fugitive and he always said it doesn't exist."

"Oh, it exists all right," said L'mak. "We've been there before. It's an amazing place, really, a village of Humans, Elves, Dwarves, Orcs, and more. It's guarded by swamps, mountains, rivers, and a clan of Orcs who are loyal to Queen Ariel. There are Borni warriors in the forest as well, to protect it. The Headman is a Human, his mate is an Elf. She's the healer."

Telee smiled at his enthusiasm. "You like it there."

"I confess I do. Everyone works together there, Orc, Elf, Human, and Dwarf. I like that."

"I would truly love to see it, but I'm weak. I doubt I'll live more than two days at most. I wasn't fed today. Tomorrow will be the second day without the oshar."

"You won't die of madness, my beloved daughter," said Tereen, once again gathering the girl into her arms. "The oshar is a poison, nothing more. As it leaves your body, you will awaken to your true self. Let me tell you how it was for me. At first ..."

While Tereen told her tale to Telee, L'mak took up his bow and took extra arrows as well as a rope. "Where are you going?" asked L'ark.

"There's too many of us, we have far to go and the weather will soon turn against us. We need supplies and we need horses. You stay here with them and guard them well, my brother. I'll go a thieving. We have fourteen with us now and only three horses."

"All right. I'll take them through the forest, but I'll travel slowly to conserve their strength. Hunt well, L'mak, return to me."

L'mak grinned and vanished into the darkness. By now the sun was starting to rise. "Tereen, rest them this day. I'll make sure you are not disturbed."

"L'ark?"

"I'll be close, my heart, but I'll make certain none find us." He too slipped away into the trees.

"Mother?"

"It's all right, I'm still getting used to it, that's all."

"Used to it? To what?"

"The Borni call the compulsion the Spirit Pull. It happens when two spirits are pulled together as one. I can feel him inside me, in my heart. The closer he is, the happier I am. At first it was painful if he went too far, but now it's changed and no longer brings such distress. Still, I like it better at his side.

"Don't worry, little one, my L'ark will protect us and bring us to safety."

"That man will come for us. The sun is up, we should run, find some place we can walk through water so the dogs can't track us."

"L'ark said to wait here, Telee. He is a Borni warrior, little one, not an escaped slave."

"Mamma, there will be many men and dogs. Even a Borni can't defeat them all. We should run."

"Hush now, sweet child. Rest now and trust. All is well."

While Tereen tried to sooth Telee and keep the others from panicking, L'ark watched from the trees as the pursuit began. The farmer had sent his sons for help in the night and there were eight men plus several hounds in the farmyard. The men shouldered their weapons and loosed the dogs.

L'ark nocked an arrow and moved back deeper into the forest. The hounds caught the scent as he leaned three more arrows against a tree. The dogs raced well ahead of the men and as they reached the trail the first one met his fate.

As the big dog yelped and fell the other dogs leaped aside, but another fell and then another. The pack turned back but still two more fell. The last dog made it back to the men and hid behind them. Angry, the men hurried on then found the dead dogs. Before they could react, an arrow took the last hound.

Fearfully they stood back to back, but they saw nothing. Before they could gather their wits, an arrow took the first man, and then another. The men scattered, but they were the hunted now. Three more fell to the bow, leaving only the original farmer and his two sons standing with their backs to a tree.

L'ark stepped out to face them, tossing aside his bow and drawing his sword. As he advanced towards them they spread out to surround him. They began to close in, then, at a barked command from the farmer, they all lunged at once. L'ark dove to the ground and rolled.

As he came back to his feet facing them he saw the farmer staring at his youngest son. The spear thrust had missed the Elf and lodged in his son's belly. Before the man could fully register what had happened L'ark's sword pierced his heart.

L'ark now faced the eldest of the sons across his father's body. "I left you alive in the forest last night. You were warned not to attempt this."

"I'll kill you, you scum sucking slave," shouted the young man, as he charged at the tall Elf. He swung his sword as hard as he could, but it struck nothing. Confused, he looked down at the dagger protruding from his chest. He died wondering how anyone could possibly move that fast.

The boy with the belly wound from his father's spear was crying for his mother. "I would take you to her, but that wound will not heal. I'm sorry for that, you were too young. I'll finish you quickly if you wish."

The boy swallowed hard and nodded. L'ark's sword was through his heart instantly. He sighed as his spirit slipped from his body, his hands falling away to expose the jagged wound in his belly.

L'ark shook his head sadly then gathered the weapons. He retrieved all his arrows as well as the weapons of the other men. He also took what coins they had and a few bits of clothing the freed Elves could use. Throwing the bundle across his shoulders L'ark set out for the camp and his beloved Tereen.

She fairly flew into his arms as he arrived and dropped his pack. "There, there, now, my beloved, all is well. The slave hunters are dead, and they've donated some clothing and weapons for us. L'mak will soon return to us with horses, so we'll be able to travel faster.

"Right now, we should move on, the weather is about to change, and I'd like to find better shelter than this clearing." He distributed the weapons and clothing, then put out the fire.

They pushed on for most of the day until L'ark found what he was looking for, a rocky overhang out of the wind. It was dry under there and many fallen leaves had blown into that large space. It would make fine bedding for them.

Tereen made a fire while L'ark went hunting. When darkness finally engulfed the world, they were enjoying a meal of venison, and Tereen was holding Telee while she listened to the wind speak of the snows to come.

A while later the rain began, pushed on by the lashing wind, yet they were warm and dry under the sheltering rocks. Telee actually smiled as she snuggled deeper into the warmth of L'ark's cloak with her mother. That smile erased many of the scars from her face, yet they returned as the smile faded.

Telee whimpered in her sleep as her mother gently stroked her brow and wept. "Oh L'ark, she's been so abused. My poor Telee was such a gentle, loving child. What have they done to her?"

"I don't know, my love, but they were harsh men, that farmer and his sons."

"I hope you killed them all."

"I did. They will torture no others. I swear it."

"What will become of her, my poor little babe? See how they have scarred her face? She was such a beautiful child."

"She still has that beauty given her by her mother," he replied softly. "I saw it as she smiled. Perhaps in her mother's loving embrace she will regain her sense of self, that sense of strength she had when she and Queen Ariel were fierce children determined to free all Elves."

"I care not for fierceness, L'ark my love, I just want her to be at peace and to smile again. She was always smiling as a child." Tereen looked up and gazed into the night, lost in a memory.

"When Ariel was forbidden to see her again, Telee pretended she had run away and been adopted by a clan of Dwarves. If she could no longer have her Elf friend she would have Dwarf friends. She used to say she would work at the forges with them until she became so strong no master would be able to beat her ever again."

L'ark smiled as he put his arm around her shoulders. "There are Dwarves in Fugitive. We'll introduce her to them. Sleep now, my treasure. I'll watch and tend the fire."

The next day L'mak returned with another six horses as well as cloaks and weapons. "We'll have to double up on the horses," he said as he sat beside the fire, "but we'll be able to make better time now."

"Rain's stopping," said L'ark. "We'll give these folks another day to rest then move out. Did you see anyone on the roads?"

"You mean besides the brigands who attacked a lone rider?" grinned L'mak.

"Yes, besides them."

"No, just them. They were so excited to see me they gave me all their cloaks, food, weapons, and horses."

"Generous folk."

"Indeed so. L'ark, we'll have to move carefully now. The robbers who normally prey on the unwary are getting desperate. Because of the queen's activities the roads are empty. They'll attack anything that moves. Alone, we could have some fun with them, but these folk aren't ready for battle yet."

"You're right there. The safety of these people is our first concern. We'll leave at first light tomorrow. You take the lead and I'll ride rear guard."

"We have a plan. So, what'll we do for fun today?"

"It's still raining and the fire's warm. It's dry here, how about language lessons?" It was agreed and thus they passed the day. The former slaves warm and dry with no work to do in the rain. Life for them was good.

THREE WEEKS LATER, as a light snow fell gently, they broke from the trees to see the houses of the Orc clan. They were greeted warmly and a runner sent on ahead. There were Humans, Elves, and Dwarves waiting to greet them at the gates of Fugitive.

They gathered at the inn where they gratefully huddled by the fire for warmth. An old Elf approached and smiled. "Good people, I am Olan, a friend. Once you're warmed and rested we'll get you all outfitted with proper winter clothes and find homes for you.

"We'll practice many things through the winter, and when the snows melt in spring, the Borni will begin teaching you how to live in and enjoy the forest. For now, you'll stay in the village. Now, which of you is Telee, friend of Lady Ariel?"

"I am, sir," she said softly, her head down fearfully.

Olan grinned. "Telee, this Dwarf is Gormin, clan chieftain of the Fugitive Dwarves. He has a task for you." She looked up with wide eyes.

The old Dwarf was grinning at her. "Hmm, you look like a sturdy lass, I think you'll do nicely. Telee, our smith, Rolfin, has need of an apprentice, but I've put all the others to work, and there's no one to take on the task. What say you? Will you help an old Dwarf out?"

"I'll do what I can, good sir. I swear I will."

"Aye then, I'll come for you in the morning."

"You'll do nothing of the sort," harrumphed one of the Dwarf women. "The poor child is half starved. She needs some time to rest and to get some food into her. I'll take her to the forge myself when she's ready."

Gormin just chuckled and winked at Telee. "Well then, the chieftain has spoken. I leave you in good hands." Still chuckling he walked away.

Two days later Telee was introduced to the smith. Rolfin wasn't all that old, but he was the most powerfully built creature Telee had ever seen, and he had the kindest eyes.

"So, ye want to be a smith, do ye? Well girl, there's not been an Elvish smith since the breaking of the world, but 'tis said they could work mighty magics with steel. All right then, ye'll be the first of a new breed. We'll start with stone."

He showed her a chunk of iron ore he took from a pile near the forge. Thus, her education began. By the time the snows melted in spring Telee was no longer the emaciated slave woman who had been brought to Fugitive, she was a powerfully built Elf who could swing a hammer with the best of them.

Demon Spawn

While L'ark was searching for Trelee, Ariel faced something new, something no Elf had ever seen before. Nearly half the procession of Elves had passed by the ruins of Elanda when Kern approached at a gallop. "My Lady Ariel, demons. Demons have attacked the front."

Ariel leaped to the saddle and followed the boy along the procession. She found the Borni, led by Mearith, in a pitched battle with wolf-like creatures. She charged into them, Grimm rearing and trampling, but she was pulled from the saddle.

Light burst from the place where she had fallen, and enemies were hurled in all directions. Ariel was back on her feet, bolts of lightning flashing from her hands, killing enemies instantly. The creatures ran from her, but she switched to her bow and brought down several more. The monsters fled into the jumbled rocks and crevasses that once had been the final battlefield of that ancient war.

Ariel was retrieving another of her arrows from the body of a beast when Mearith reached her and swept her into loving arms. "Ariel, are you harmed?"

"I'm fine, my heart. Oh, my love, you're wounded."

"A few scrapes only, my delight."

Ariel gently released herself from Mearith's embrace. "What are these things, Mearith my heart?"

"I've not seen such things before in all my long years. By their looks they were once wolves, or Ogres who were misshapen by magics gone wrong. The Geni, growing desperate at the end, began some terrible experiments in their efforts to create more warriors. Perhaps these are descended from some such."

Ariel sighed deeply as she retrieved yet another arrow. "How many did we lose?" she asked.

"Unknown at the moment. Arlon is approaching as we speak. He'll have the answer for you, my delight."

Ariel nodded and whistled for Grimm. The big war horse pranced over to her, and she began to inspect him for wounds. There were a few scratches and plenty of blood, none his. She hugged his neck then released him as Arlon reached her.

"My queen."

"How bad is it, Arlon?"

"Better than we had a right to expect, my Lady. We have two dead Borni, seven dead Bornani, and a number of wounds. Beren is busy with the wounded, but she said most would recover."

"Most?"

"There are some bad wounds. Sadly, those will slow us down as the wounded will have to be carried. I've sent out scouts to keep an eye out for more of these things. Do you know what they are, Lady?"

"No. Lady Mearith believes they're the results of Geni experiments gone wrong. Here comes Tanis and Trelanth. Perhaps she can shed some light on this for us."

"My queen, I have failed you."

"Trelanth?"

"Ethor, the man who was tasked with keeping us hidden from prying eyes, was the first attacked. His concentration was broken for only moments, but it was enough. The Geni are aware of us now. I have them blocked again, but I can feel them focusing their power, several working together. Lady, they may well break past me in time."

Ariel began to pace, her mind racing. Suddenly she stopped. "Let them see me, Trelanth. Let them see me surrounded by Borni warriors and mages."

Trelanth grinned her delight. "Do you wish to speak to them?"

"Oh yes, let them hear me as well."

The mage sank to the ground and began breathing deeply. Ariel stepped out, her body suddenly glowing with power. At Trelanth's nod she let her vision seek the Geni. She saw several of them gathered about a ball of polished crystal.

"So, you wish to see your doom approach, do you, invaders?" Ariel's voice sounded hollow, harsh, as though spoken from another realm. "Well then, look upon me and my warriors. We are nearly at the gates of Shotar. We will come, and as your armies were before, you will be swept aside. The Elves of Elanda have returned for vengeance."

A flick of her hand and Trelanth broke the spell. Once again, they were hidden from prying eyes. "Well?"

Trelanth's vision was focused far away. Suddenly she grinned. "They no longer seek us, my queen. They're now in a panic. It appears they're trying to reinforce the gates and fortifications."

Ariel sighed and let her shoulders sag. "Well, that should entertain them long enough for us to reach Narthwood."

"Lady, they will now recall all their forces from the south," said Arlon.

"I know, but what else could I do? Mearith, what think you?"

"If, as you say, the Geni fear the cold, they won't be in a hurry to march north in winter. I expect they'll spend their efforts shoring up the city."

"Yes, and that led to the downfall of my people so long ago. Perhaps it will become the undoing of the Geni as well. While they prepare for a battle at the gates of Shotar, we'll strike at another city which has been emptied to defend their stronghold.

"We made a mistake leaving Magdan untouched. We should have burned it to the ground."

"Perhaps, my delight."

"No, Mearith my heart, listen, we have wounded with us, and that will slow us down as some of our resources are diverted to tend and transport them, yes?"

"That is true, my delight. What are you thinking?"

"They'll pull the greater share of their resources back to defend Shotar. That army will have to be fed and housed. Now, imagine if a thousand or more refugees suddenly appear at the gates. They too will have to be fed and housed as well as protected from marauding Elvish armies."

Both Mearith and Arlon grinned. "And if they refuse the refugees, they weaken their position. As well, we might possibly gain allies. My delight, I begin to see your reasoning. However, first we have to get our army to Narthwood."

"We do. Arlon, the time for teaching has passed. Every able-bodied Elf in this army now has to take up arms and get some practical experience. Enough woodcraft has been learned for that."

"Indeed, it has, my queen. Most are now fairly adept in the forest. Much more needs to be learned, but perhaps now is the time to practice what has already been taught."

"Indeed. Spread the word, Arlon my friend. Speed up the march with as many as you can. Mearith and I will ride rear guard. Keep scouts out on all sides, but get them running. When you reach Evanseth take your Borni and return for us."

"My Lady?"

"Do it, Arlon. I now must deal with the reality that faces me. Not all will survive. I'll remain at rear guard to ensure as many as possible do so."

"Tanis, you will take the Guard with Arlon."

"My queen, should not the Royal Guard remain with the monarch?"

He was grinning and she smiled as she gripped his shoulder. "Tanis, I want you to survive."

"My Lady, a guard that leaves their queen behind is a poor guard indeed. Lady, please, we belong at your side. As mighty as you and Lady Mearith are, you are only two, and this day we were attacked by dozens."

"He's right, my queen," said Arlon. "I'll leave a score of my best with you as well."

"And I too will stay," said Trelanth. Ariel arched an eyebrow at her, but the girl just grinned. "Arlon will have three mages with him, you should have at least one."

"She's right, my delight," grinned Mearith. Ariel smiled and nodded her acquiescence. "All right then, let's get moving. The longer we stand here planning, the more vulnerable we become. Arlon, get them up, get them moving."

Tanis was already on his feet and running. In mere moments Ariel was surrounded by her guard. All were mounted. Ariel was surprised at how fast the Borni sprang to life.

They trotted past her, most of the Bornani with them. As the main group got moving it began to pick up speed. She was surprised to see many grinning faces as they sped past her. The Bornani might not be as great warriors as the Borni, and they still had much to learn, but they were more than equal to a hard run through the forest after weeks on the trail.

Once the runners had vanished along the path, Ariel saw her much smaller party form up. There were the wounded and a few who'd stayed behind to help the healer and tend to the wounded. They set out with a Borni warrior leading while the rest of the warriors slipped into the forest to scout for trouble.

Mearith and Ariel rode close behind their small group, Tanis and the guard beside them. When they finally camped for the night there was no sign of the Borni and Bornani runners.

When the next day dawned, they continued, albeit at a slower pace. Two days later snow began to fall. Ariel sighed as she rode along beside Mearith, who spoke softly. "Beren seems troubled, shall we investigate?"

The queen nodded and urged her horse forward. "Beren, what news?"

"My supply of herbs is running low, Lady. I fear they will be long gone before we arrive at Elfhome. I cannot gather more now the snow is falling."

"Understood. Do the best you can, Beren. No more can you do. Mearith, dear heart, are we not near a village?"

"We are. It's the first of the four we encounter on our way to Narthwood."

"The path around this one is rather steep, is it not?"

"Ariel, what are you suggesting?"

"The Geni already know we didn't go south. What harm could it do?"

"Well, they didn't have time to recall the troops from the south, and they are busy fortifying the city, I guess there's no real harm in sending them a few refugees. However, if we do this, they will know we've gone north."

"Evanseth has our people well to the north of here. It would take an army weeks to reach that place and they'd have a lot of rough terrain to cross before that. There will be slaves in that village, and a healer with the supplies Beren needs. What think you, my beloved?"

"I'd like to have a look at the place for myself. Perhaps I can raid the apothecary's shop first, if there is one."

"And the slaves?"

"To free the slaves, we'll have to be a bit more heavy-handed. Are you planning to hit every town and village between here and Narthwood?"

"Do they have slaves?"

Mearith grinned. "I believe they do. Since that is our quest, to free all the slaves, should we bring them with us?"

"Let's do."

It was mid-day and most of the village folk were at the inn, huddled by the fire to stay warm. Suddenly a man burst through the door. "Riders coming in, warriors by the look of them."

The village headman rose to his feet, alarmed. "Warriors? Here? How many?"

"Two dozen or more," panted the man, as he tried to regain his breath.

"What do they want here?"

"I don't know, you ask them."

"Perhaps they just want a place to wait out the storm," said someone.

"Aye, and maybe they're another group of brigands looking for booty. Arm yourselves." Everyone swept up whatever they could for a weapon and followed him out to the yard. The horsemen were just appearing from the swirling snows. "Hold right there. Who are you and what do you want here?"

"Is there an apothecary in this fair town?" called one of the riders. "Our healer is in need of supplies."

"Janine may have something," replied the man. "She'll want payment in coin."

"Coin she shall have," replied the rider, still drawing closer.

The headman shivered and not from the cold. That cloaked rider was atop a massive war horse. That beast alone could trample the village into dust. He turned and spoke to the man nearest to him. That man hurried off to fetch the healer.

Nervously the headman watched as the riders fanned out to command all the open space in the village square. All were heavily armed, but hidden within the dark cloaks. No one made a sound that might alarm them.

A woman was soon dragged reluctantly before the riders. "What do you want?" she asked, trying to hide behind the headman.

"Our healer needs supplies. We'll pay in coin."

"All right, follow me." The lead rider waved an arm and a woman dismounted to follow. "Beren, get as much as she can spare." The woman nodded. As she was led away another rider mounted on a black warhorse followed.

The lead rider spoke again. "Headman, the one who follows the healer is Mearith the Merciless. If there is any treachery afoot ..."

"No, no, there's no treachery. We're honest folk here, we don't harm anybody, and we have nothing of value."

"That remains to be seen. First the medical supplies. Ah, here she comes now. Beren, how goes it?"

"The apothecary was well supplied, my queen. I have more than enough to get us to our destination."

"Excellent. Kern, take her back to the main encampment." A youth on a fast-looking horse came forward and swept the healer, full sack and all, up behind him then disappeared into the falling snows.

The one who had been addressed as the queen tossed a bag of coins to the apothecary who looked inside then gave a cry of delight. "Are you satisfied with the payment?" The woman bobbed her head then hurried away before the rider could change her mind.

"Now then, Headman, for the rest of our business."

"The rest of our business?" He swallowed hard and gripped his old sword tighter.

"Yes, I offer you a bargain and I suggest you take it." She reached up and swept back her hood. An Elf. Again, he tried to swallow the fear in his throat, but it stuck there.

"I am Ariel, Queen of all Elves. The forest is my home and my realm. Bring forth all the slaves held in this village and release them to me. Do this and no harm will come to any of you. Refuse me and I will take them by force, kill every living person here, and then burn the village to the ground.

"Release your slaves to me, never hold another Elf slave, and we'll pass you by. In future, we may come to trade or for other business, but we will always pay our way in full as long as there are no slaves here. This is the bargain, what say you?"

Another man stepped forward, anger in his posture and his voice. "We won't just hand over the slaves to you. How would we survive the winter? How could we tend our farms? No, I say no ..."

He suddenly grabbed his throat and tried to draw breath. The queen had reached out a hand and closed it into a fist. "This land was once the domain of the High Born Elves, and I was their queen. I have returned to reclaim what was stolen from me, and that includes my people."

She released him and he fell to the ground gasping in as much air as he could. She dismounted and strode to the center of the square then held up her arms. Fire leaped from her hands to surround her, slowly enveloping her and expanding until the headman was forced to step back from the heat. With a wave of her hand the fire vanished.

"Bring all the slaves to me here within the turning of the glass or pay the price. Move!"

The villagers scattered and in short order nearly a dozen slaves were brought to her. "Where are the children? The pregnant females? I want them all. Do you hear?" Fire leaped skyward from her hands again. "I want them all; I want them now."

The rest of the slaves were soon before her in the square. They stood trembling in the falling snow, terrified. "Be at peace, my brothers and sisters," she said kindly. "Are all here now? All the slaves in the village?"

"Yes, all are here, Lady," replied one woman, ducking her head deferentially. Her eyes darted furtively to a man at the edge of the square, but Ariel saw it. So did Mearith.

That man groaned and sank to the ground, a dagger in his shoulder. Horrified, he watched as the big black war horse paced toward him. "When the queen gives an order, it is best to obey," said a cold deadly voice. "Bring the rest and quickly." Clutching his tunic to his wound he hurried away.

"Are there any others holding back?" asked Ariel. There was a swift round of denials.

Ariel looked at the slave woman who'd lied. "The truth now, my sister, how many did he hold back?"

Tears streamed down her face. "My child. His brother will have killed her by now."

"If that happens, I swear to you he and his brother will pay with their lives then I'll burn this accursed village to the ground."

A few moments later the wounded man returned with a small child. Mearith didn't speak, but she wiped her blade on the man's cloak. She swept the child into her arms and leaped aboard her horse.

Ariel waved her arm and the rest of her riders came forward and took up a slave behind them then slowly rode away, vanishing into the falling snow.

"The king will hear of this," came a voice from the gathered folk.

Ariel smiled as she leaped back to the saddle. "I've no doubt he will. Shotar isn't so far away, if you have need perhaps the king might share some of his bounty with you this winter.

"Hear me well, people. We paid in coin for the medicines we needed, and in future we will pay for whatever else we might need. My people will always bargain fairly, but we're not slaves, and we will set free every slave we encounter. Know this. Expect us to return at odd times, for we will be patrolling these forests in future."

She tossed another bag of coins to the headman. Startled, he looked up to see her smile. "You've had an exciting day. Buy a round of ale for all at my expense." With that she wheeled her charger and left the square. By the time darkness fell, the snows had hidden all their tracks, but then, no one would have wanted to follow them anyway.

Back at the camp, Beren was tending the wounded while Tanis did his best to convince the former slaves the collars were off forever. Ariel was gazing up at the sky, not liking what she was seeing. The voice of the wind didn't bring her any comfort either.

"Ariel, my delight, we must be on the move. The weather will set in all too soon, and we're too exposed here."

She nodded. "Agreed," she replied softly. "Quickly now, my heart, find us shelter from the storm if you can." Mearith tossed her the reins and leaped to the ground to vanish into the trees and gathering gloom. Darkness had fallen before she returned.

Ariel approached Beren and began to assist her. "My queen, I fear the storm is worsening."

"I know. Mearith seeks a safe haven even as we speak. We must get them ready to travel." Beren nodded and they set about the task. It was made more difficult by the newly freed starting to panic. They'd been taken from the only shelter they'd ever known and whisked off into the forest.

Worse yet, there was no oshar to eat, the young warrior said they would be happier without it, but as darkness fell and hunger settled in, they began to doubt. The group set out slowly as day darkened into night, and with the stoicism of the slave, they trudged along.

Darkness settled onto the silent forest, but they didn't stop. The queen and her troops seemed to be able to see in the dark. A shadow appeared from the gloom and called out. "This way, quickly now, this way." Without a pause in her stride the queen turned to follow the shadow.

A soft glow soon appeared then the track led into a huge cavern where a cheery fire crackled and snapped. "Get another fire going some ways from that one," said Mearith. "Borni, help me find more wood for the fire. This storm will be a bad one."

Ariel gathered a few sticks of wood together then snapped her fingers. As the wood burst into flames, she noticed Mearith watching her. "We have wounded and newly freed, there's no time to wait for it to catch and grow." She threw another dried branch on the blaze then reached to help a wounded man closer to the warmth. Mearith nodded, then stepped outside to gather more wood.

When the light of day returned, the storm was in full rage. The wind shrieked and howled around the entrance to the cave, occasionally sending flurries of snow inside. "We have barely enough wood to last the day and a night," said Ariel. "Will it blow out so soon, do you think?"

"I do, my delight. Ariel ..."

"I know, dear heart, I know. I used a lot of magic yesterday, relying on that instead of the things you've taught me. I know this troubles you. Will you hear my reasoning?"

"Of course. Ariel, I don't mean to chastise you, I just ..."

"I know, my love, I know. Listen to me now. I did what I did yesterday to free the slaves without a battle. We already have wounded with us. Also, I have an idea, a piece of the vision Queen Onlay showed me, her vision of the future. She showed me villages like that one, but with Humans, Elves, Orcs, and Dwarves all working and living peacefully together.

"I saw in those people a possible beginning of that dream. If we slaughter them all to free the Elves, that can never happen."

"And so you frightened them, but harmed no one. I begin to see the reasoning. And the fire?"

"All right, I was in a hurry and got lazy," sighed Ariel. "Happy now?"

"I'm always happy when you're near."

"Nice recovery," grinned Ariel, as she gently poked Mearith in the ribs with a finger.

"Now, my delight, it's your turn," said Mearith. "Tell me what's on your mind."

"We have three more villages like the last between us and the open lands that mark the edge of Narthwood, do we not?"

"Indeed, we do. So, you want to empty them all of slaves as we pass by."

"Can we, Mearith? It'll break my heart to leave them behind."

"I know, my delight, I know."

Mearith looked thoughtful, almost sad. Ariel relented and put an arm around her shoulder, hugging her gently. "If I forswear the use of magic unless there is no other option, will you smile for me?"

"You know me so well, Ariel. Please understand, I have no compunction about using magical means to meet our ends ..."

"But you're afraid I'll fall under the spell of the power as did my ancestors."

"It is true, my delight. I fear for you, for I love you beyond measure."

"Let me tell you something Onlay told me. There were many generations before me, any one of which could have awakened to the power, as I did, for the opportunities were there. She told me that the power waited for me, she waited for me, until you were ready to return to Elandor."

"Oh? Did she say more?"

"Yes. She said that the strength of both were needed to succeed, the strength to wield the power lies in me, but the strength to hold me in this world, to keep me focused, lies in you.

"My heart, I know that if the Bornani see me doing everything with magic they will follow my example. They'll expect me to do everything for them and gain no self-reliance. The resulting disaster of that path came to me in a dream last night. She showed it to me. I fully understand I must demonstrate to them it can be done without the use of the high power.

"I'll leave the magic to Trelanth and company from now on. Now your mightiest task begins."

"Oh?"

"You made me a queen, now you must truly make me queen of the forest."

"Oh my delight, you have already mastered the ways of the forest."

"Stop now, you know better than that. If I'm to forsake the high power then I must know and automatically reach for the forest magic, the more natural way for an Elf. Teach me."

"I will, my love, I will. Look, the storm seems to be abating. Here comes Beren."

"Beren, what troubles you?" asked Ariel.

The girl sighed as she sank to the ground before her queen. "Lady, I fear many of those with us will never reach Elfhome."

"Oh?"

"Lady, is there no way to travel faster? The sooner we reach the healing skills of the elder Elves the better their chances of survival. I do what I can, but ..."

"I do understand, Beren, I do. Perhaps it's time to take a more direct approach. Send Tanis and Trelanth to me. We'll devise a way to get things moving again."

"Thank you, my queen."

Beren rose and sought out Trelanth and Tanis who hurried to Ariel's side. "Trelanth, see what you can do to spy out any pursuit or danger along the road. Tanis, ready your troops. We will soon arrive at another village. I want the slaves freed and waiting for us when we arrive."

With a grin of delight, he leaped to his feet and raced out into the snows, calling to the rest of the guard to follow. "Ariel?"

"You have the right of it, my heart," she sighed, as she leaned her head on Mearith's shoulder. "Queen Onlay sent the dream to show me the folly of doing it all myself, even though I now have the power to do so. No, it's my task to lead them, it's their task to free their brothers and sisters themselves.

"That was the message of the dream, we must free them, yes, but that alone will not be enough. We must also make them strong again, as they once were so long ago. If I stray from that path again, remind me of this day."

"I will, sweet Ariel, I will."

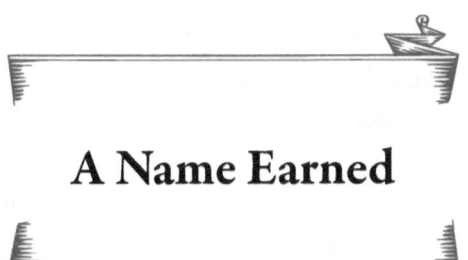

A Name Earned

While Ariel slowly realized the meaning and the lesson of her dream, far away in Fugitive, another Elf also had a dream. Telee had taken to sleeping near the forge. Instead of being chained in a damp cellar at night, she was now warmed by the hot coals in the forge, there were no chains, and the door was left open a crack so she could look out at the sky.

On this day, the smith found her hard at work, the forge already glowing in the winter air. He smiled sadly as he saw her there, stripped to the waist, sweat glistening on her badly scarred back. "Telee, how are ye?" he asked by way of greeting. "What're ye working on before the sun's up?"

"Rolfin, sorry, I didn't hear you approach," she replied hastily, her eyes downcast.

He smiled warmly and patted her arm. "Easy, girl, I meant no censure, just curiosity."

She sighed and smiled as she met his warm grin. "I'll get used to it, Rolfin, I will. I know you meant no censure. I'll work extra to pay for the iron, but please let me do this."

"Forget the iron, lass. Tell me what you're up to, maybe I can help."

Again, she sighed. "It came to me in a dream, he came to me in a dream. An Elf with old eyes and arms like a Dwarven smith. He was working at the forge, and he spoke to me. "It's up to you to remember what we all once knew. First you must make a sword, then learn to use it. Here's what you do.""

"Rolfin, he showed me how to make a sword like I've never seen before. Even the Borni don't have them, at least none I've seen do."

"This man, what did he look like? Was there anyone at the forge with him?"

"He was tall, but broad and heavily muscled, and bearded like a Dwarf. Yes, I think there was someone with him there, a Dwarf was there."

"Ah, so that's it then. Telee, there's an old legend among my people, a tale of two smiths, Dwarf and Elf. Together they worked magic with the steel, made mighty weapons, the like which have not been seen in the world since before time began.

"So, he spoke of this, did he? Do you remember the process?"

"Yes, most of it. Rolfin, please let me try this. It felt so real, that dream."

"Aye, a god-sent dream will seem that way. All right girl, but let me help ye. Let's see if Elf and Dwarf can bring to life the old magic of forge and hammer. You direct, what do we do first?"

And so it began. The days and weeks rolled by, and every chance they had they worked on the sword. The metal was heated, folded, folded, and folded over again. The winter was well along when it was finished.

Through the process Telee had several dreams, each showing her the next step in the process, teaching her the rune songs to sing as she worked. Her sweet lilt accompanied by Rolfin's deep bass could be heard from the forge, and people would often stop to listen.

It was the way of the people in Fugitive that everyone trained with weapons, and Telee had been no different. Each day they had practiced, and the day her sword was finished she got to put that practice into motion.

Telee and Rolfin stood admiring the long slim blade as she continued to polish it until it gleamed in the sun. They had sung the runes into it and stamped them onto it. She had named it Blooddrinker and that name was also on the blade in Dwarven runes.

"Ye'll polish it until there's nothing left," grinned Rolfin. Just then the alarm sounded. Pigmen were attacking.

Without a thought, or stopping to grab her tunic, Telee raced to the walls, the winter sun gleaming off the pale skin of her upper body. She leaped up the steps to help push a ladder away then leaped over into the mass of attackers below.

With a roar, Rolfin was over the wall beside her. He stopped in amazement as he watched her fight. This wasn't the frail Elf slave girl they'd asked him to befriend, this was a hard-muscled smith wielding a magic sword of her own making.

All the rage and defiance she had harbored against her masters was released as she fought with a berserk madness. The Blooddrinker sliced through weapon, armor, body, and bone as though through butter. Nothing could stand before her and, as Drakkat arrived with Marc, the pigmen turned and fled the mad Elvish warrior.

Still screaming her hate at them, Telee ran down several more before she stopped, her arms hanging at her sides, her blade red with blood. Great heaving sobs escaped her as she drew as much air into her lungs as possible.

She was exhausted and shivering in the cold when they reached her. Marc swept his warm cloak around her shoulders as Rolfin steadied her. "Damned greedy Elf," rumbled Drakkat, as he grinned at her. "You could have saved a few for us to play with."

Telee looked to see his grin of approval as he offered his hand and took her wrist in the warrior's grip. "You'd have made a fine Orc," he chuckled. She smiled weakly then fainted into his arms. He scooped her up easily and headed for the gate. "The inn?"

"The forge," replied Rolfin. "She'll feel safe there when she awakens. I'll bring her to the inn for food as soon as she comes around." He carried her back and gently laid her on her sleeping pallet, the now clean and gleaming sword at her hand. He was sitting beside her as she awakened.

"What happened? Where are the pigmen?"

"They ran away," he grinned. "Some mad berserk Elf warrior leaped over the wall and slaughtered half of them, and the rest ran away."

"Rolfin?"

"What possessed ye, girl, to do a thing like that?"

"I don't know," she said as she sat up. "I saw them, and then they weren't pigmen anymore."

"Oh?"

"No. I saw them change. What I saw was master and his sons, the old master, the Geni, Orcs, men, ..."

"Aye, I thought there was far too much rage there for the pigmen. So, you fought and slew your oppressors?"

"Yes. I killed them all. I let free all the pain and hate from inside me, I repaid the blows, the rapes, the hot irons, all of it. From the day I was taken away from Ariel, I was beaten, tortured, and more.

"Rolfin, that wasn't me who fought them, it was somebody else from inside me. She had no fear, she felt no pain, she just killed and killed and killed. When I was too tired to lift my arms, and they were all gone, she retreated inside me again.

"I know she's in there, and she scares me."

"Let it be, lass. Let it be. That's the tired talking now. Come, we'll be off to the inn for a feed and a pint. You've earned it this day."

He helped her to stand then led her to the inn. She pulled on her old tunic and slung the sword across her back. When they entered, she returned Marc's cloak to him and sat to the table, shyly looking down at her hands.

"Here, Freida," said the Dwarf woman who served her. "Eat this, it'll restore your strength and put hair on your chest."

"What did you call me?"

"Freida. There's an old legend of a Dwarf woman who worked at the forge and fought beside the men in battle. It's a better name for you. Telee was a slave, but you're that no longer. You're a warrior and a smith now, and you'd make a fine Dwarf."

"It's a tradition among the Dwarves," smiled Rolfin. "A young warrior must earn his name. I think Freida suits you, what do you say, will you wear it?"

Tears filled her eyes as she looked at all the smiling faces. "I don't know what to say. I ..."

"They're right," said Tereen. "My poor Telee was too abused, and can never be who she was, I know that now. However, my fierce daughter, Freida, who works at the forge with the Dwarves, she is another story. She could never be made slave; none could ever bend her to the collar. She'd never bow to the whip."

"So, girl, what do you say? 'Tis a powerful name they offer," said Gormin. "It's a name that carries a lot of honor. Could be tough to live up to." He was grinning at her like a proud father. "Go on, child, take up the name and the challenge."

"You people are all crazy, and I love you for it. Perhaps you're right. I've worn many names over the years, and perhaps it's time for a new one. All right, Freida it is. I am now Freida, the Smith of Fugitive.

"Olan, what are you smiling about?"

"I was just thinking of how proud the queen would be of her childhood friend. She often said you had the heart of a warrior, and she always expected that you'd be the first to escape and free the other."

Freida smiled shyly, then noticed L'ark eying her sword. "May I see it?" he asked. She nodded and passed it over.

L'ark hefted the blade, turning it this way and that in his hand before returning it to her. "I confess I never expected to hold such a blade again."

"L'ark?"

"Long ago, well before the time of the Orcs and Humans arrival in Elandor, the great smiths of the High Born made such weapons. Nearly all had passed into the mystery of time before I was born. Once, a prince of Elanda showed one he kept on the wall of his villa. It had been in his family for many generations.

"All knowledge of its making had vanished into the mists of time by then. You made this?"

"Rolfin and I together, yes."

"Could you make more?"

"I believe so, Rolfin?"

"Aye, I believe we could, but it's taken the better part of the winter to make the Blooddrinker. They're not so easy to make."

L'ark smiled and nodded. "I thought as much. In the legends of Freida, she wielded a sword of her own making, a sword like no other, a magic sword, forged in the god fire, and sung into being with mighty runes of making.

"The name suits you, girl, and I for one am happy to have you here to help us defend Fugitive."

"L'ark, do you want me to make you a sword like this?"

"No, girl. A sword that can never know defeat would be too tempting for a simple soldier like me. No, I think yours should be the only one, and that only you should have it, for I doubt any other could master it. It came into being by your hand, and I fully expect it's your hand alone that can wield it."

There was a round of agreement at that, and she sat amazed at both what had happened, and the reaction of these people to it. Any of her former masters would have taken it for themselves and commanded her to make more to sell.

She smiled wistfully and allowed the stew to warm her insides while the love and acceptance of these people warmed her heart. Freida the Smith had found her true home at last.

As she sat by the fire, savoring the sound of her new name, the door banged open and three men entered. "Marc, we've cleared up the mess Telee made," grinned one fellow.

"Her name's Freida now," replied Marc. "So, did they leave us anything useful?"

"No. They came in through the forest to avoid the Orc village, but the strange thing is, how they got past the Borni."

L'ark sat up straighter. "That's bothering me as well. How did a war band of pigmen manage to slip past the Borni?"

"No idea," replied the man, as he lowered himself to a bench, "but they were all wearing these." He tossed an amulet onto the rough table.

As the amulet hit the table Freida's sword began to glow and throb with a soft light. She reached over with it to touch the object which hissed and began to melt. L'ark started to swear. "L'mak, you know what that is."

"I do. I'll fetch the rest and bring them here." With that he rose and bolted through the door.

"L'ark, talk to me," said Marc.

"These things were worn by the demons the Geni released at the breaking of the world. With one of these a man is invisible until he strikes a blow. If they all had them they could walk right up to the walls unseen. It wasn't until they put up ladders and started to climb that they were noticed."

"I'm not happy with the sound of that," said Marc.

"Nor am I," growled Drakkat. "So, how do we combat this, L'ark?"

"We need a mage, but we don't have one, nor can we get one until the queen returns. What we have to do now is change how we operate."

"Agreed," said Marc. "They avoided the Orcs. Is that because they could see them?"

"Yes, the fetish only worked against Elves. Men, Orcs, and Dwarves were unaffected."

"So we switch," said Drakkat. "Men, Dwarves, and Orcs must do the forest patrols and the Borni defend Fugitive from inside, at least until the queen returns in spring."

Randall had been sitting by the fire, warming his old bones and listening. He smiled to himself and nodded. "Randall, what have we missed?" asked Marc. "That grin of yours tells me we missed something important. What was it?"

"We already have our mage," he grinned in reply. "The mage of the forge. Freida's sword came right to life when that thing was brought through the door. As soon as it hit the table the sword wanted to destroy it. Am I right, Freida?"

"Yes," she replied. "I felt like it wanted me to smash it."

"So tell me, Mage of the Forge, could you make something small with the same process as the sword. Nothing big or elaborate, just a small trinket for each Elf to carry that would warn him of the pigmen's approach?"

"I don't know? I think I could. Rolfin?"

"Oh aye, no trouble to pour the metal, but we'll have to sing it to life. Perhaps if we made a long bar and sang to it, then cut it down to smaller bits. It might work. Have ye got any more of those damned things? We'll need one to use as a test." The man fished another fetish from his pocket and tossed it to him.

"What else, Randall?" asked Marc.

"Do you really want to try bringing all those forest runners and keep them inside walls for the rest of the winter? L'ark gets twitchy after a couple of days."

There was a round of laughter at that. "You're right, as usual, old friend. All right, perhaps it's better if we send a few Humans and Orcs to the Borni. They can spy out the pigmen and the Borni can watch for the rest. Freida can defend the village."

Another round of laughter that made her blush filled the room. "Ah, Marc's right," said Gormin. "With Freida here the Dwarves can easily hold the village from within."

"We're still overlooking one obvious problem," growled Drakkat. "Where did those porkers get the fetishes from? If they found them, that's one thing. If they've learned to make them, that's another."

"That's a problem for you to solve," said Freida, as she rose to her feet. "Rolfin and I have our task, and we should begin. Gormin, a second forge will need to be built. If we're to be making counter fetishes, someone else will have to make the plowshares, mend the harness, ..."

"Aye, I understand, girl. I've a fair hand with a hammer, I'll build a forge beside your own and get to work at it myself. We'll leave these tall folk to run about in the deep snows." With that, he grinned and winked at her. They left the inn together.

For the next cycle of the moon, Freida worked at the forge from before sunup until well after dark. The sweet lilt of her voice coupled with Rolfin's deep bass sang to the beat and ring of the hammers.

In the forest, young Humans and Orcs accompanied the Borni patrols. Several times the pigmen tried to return, but each time they were spotted and driven back. As spring began to approach, every Borni had a new talisman around their neck, it was a small steel disk with a tree stamped on it. The tree glowed red if an enemy was near.

Even with the new disks, the Borni asked to keep the young scouts with them, and they readily agreed. A bond of friendship was growing among the races of Fugitive. As Drakkat often said, it was a good thing.

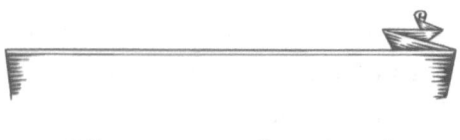

Clearing the Path

The day dawned clear and sunny. As the villagers began to move about they saw riders approaching out of the south. With the sun glaring off the fresh snow the people were nearly blinded and couldn't tell who or what was approaching.

As they reached the village square, the riders fanned out and drew bows, placing an arrow at the ready. The lead rider walked his horse to the small group of people who were gathering. His face was hidden within the hood he'd pulled forward to shade his eyes.

Fearfully, a man stepped towards the rider. "Who are you and what do you want here?"

The rider pushed back his hood. It was a young Elf. "I'm Tanis, captain of the queen's guard. I want your slaves, all of them."

"What? Well, you can't have them."

"Perhaps I should put this another way," smiled Tanis. "If you give up the slaves, all of them, without a fight, then no one gets hurt. Further, in future Elves will visit your village to buy and trade fairly. In this way, all will prosper."

"Why would we need you, we sell our goods in Shotar, and how would we manage without the slaves? Don't be foolish, boy. Send your master to me and we'll ..."

With a flick of his wrist, Tanis sent a dagger into the man's arm. "Fool. If my queen arrives here and there are no freed slaves waiting for her, she'll burn the place to the ground. Bring out the slaves or we'll kill the lot of you and take them anyway."

A spear streaked towards him, but Tanis twisted in the saddle and the spear flew harmlessly past him. There was a thud and a groan as the man who threw the spear fell with an arrow in his chest. Two more men who'd reached for weapons fell and everyone ran for cover.

"Hear me," shouted Tanis. "Bring all your slaves to me now. If you don't I'll start killing, and I'll take a life for every time a whip touched my back. I'll take three for my mother who was slain before my eyes to teach me obedience. At a count of ten, Elves had better be standing before me."

He turned in the saddle and called out to his companions. "Three of you ready torches. At ten we'll start burning the huts." Before he could say more an arrow struck his back, but it fell away harmlessly, the shield he had slung across his back beneath the cloak, protected him.

"So, you've chosen to fight. Burn the first three." There were screams of protest, and cries for mercy as two half-starved Elves were hustled from the huts and shoved at him. They stood trembling beside his horse.

The village was a war zone now, women and children ran screaming from the huts, seeking shelter in the trees. The Elves moved far too fast and were deadly with the bows as well as with their swords. When a village man closed with them he found them too strong and fast to fight.

Suddenly it stopped as the remaining men threw down their weapons. Seven more slaves were herded out to the rider who had not moved. He looked down at the frightened slaves and spoke. "Is this all of you?"

"Master?"

"I'm not your master, nor will you ever have one again. My name is Tanis. Tell me truly now, are there more slaves in the village?"

"Two more, Master. A farm about a mile away, that way." It was a young woman who spoke and pointed with a shaking hand.

"Do you know the path?"

"Yes, Master."

"Tanis, remember? Just Tanis." He turned in the saddle and called out. "Korath, there are two more at a nearby farm. Take another with you and retrieve them. This woman can guide you."

She watched fearfully as two warriors leaped to the saddle and approached. Silently one reached a hand toward her, and she was pulled easily onto the horse behind him. "Point the way," came a gentle voice. She pointed and they set out.

Tanis turned and faced the cowering villagers. "Give me one reason to leave you alive." No one spoke. "Listen carefully. Take your wounded inside and care for them. Bring to me cloaks, boots, tunics, and leggings for these Elves. Do it now and I'll spare the rest of the village. Move!"

The few village men still standing hurried to obey. Tanis dismounted, and, to the shocked surprise of the slaves, he used his dagger to remove their collars. "I promise you, my brothers and sisters, you will never wear the collar again."

"Are you going to kill us?"

He grinned as he replied. "Actually, I thought I'd take you with me. The queen will be along soon and then we'll all go on together."

"Where are you taking us?"

"We'll take you to a place far from here where there are no slaves, a place where you can live in peace."

Tears streamed down the older woman's face. "Can it be true, is there such a place?"

"There is, my sister. Do you know the tales of the Borni of the forest?"

"Yes."

"That's where we're going. The queen is taking us to Elfhome. The Borni are there, and so are the Bornani. That's who we are, the freed slaves. The Borni teach us to live free and we become the Bornani, the Children of the Forest.

"Here come the clothes. Dress yourselves warmly, good people, for we have far to go."

"Then you'd better leave me here, Master Tanis," said the older woman. "I won't be able to make a long trip. I'll just be a burden to you. I'm too old."

To her surprise, he swept the cloak from his back and snugged it around her shoulders. "Stay warm, good woman, and have no fear, we won't leave you behind."

He looked up to see smoke in the distance. Korath was returning, leading his horse which had two riders. The other horse had only one rider and was also being led by a member of the guard. "Korath, success?"

"Success, Tanis."

"Excellent. Move our new friends back beside one of the burning huts, it'll be warmer there for them. Make up some tea and give them something to eat. We'll settle in to await the queen's arrival.

"All you villagers, get inside now and remain there until our people have passed through."

About two hours later the queen's party was seen approaching. The villagers peeking out of their huts saw over fifty hardened warriors escorting a wagon and a number of wounded. The man Tanis knelt to the woman on the giant horse and spoke. "All is as you requested, my queen."

"Rise, Tanis," she smiled. "I am well pleased with you. I can see that you had to be somewhat persuasive in releasing our people."

"It was a troublesome negotiation, Lady, but we succeeded in the end."

"I see our new folk are well dressed for travel. Well done, my friend. Let's be on our way, for there is much daylight left, and I would be on the march."

Tanis grinned, then turned and fairly tossed the older woman into the saddle of his horse. "Keep that saddle warm for me," he grinned. "I need to stretch my legs."

With Ariel leading the way they set out on the road. Another village before them, then two more days to reach the open plains that stood guard before Narthwood. With luck, Arlon would be waiting for them there.

WHEN THEY CAMPED FOR the night Ariel spoke with the newly free slaves and told them of what she had planned for them. She offered them free choice then, and they all begged to go with her.

Trelanth helped Beren to bind their hurts then explained why there was no oshar, and what would happen when it left their system. Ariel watched and smiled.

Mearith leaned closer and spoke. "Are you certain of this, dear heart?"

"He did well this day, did he not?"

"He did that, and perhaps you're right about this. They faced superior numbers, yet they came away with only a few scrapes to show for the battle. All right, if you're certain. It's a mighty task you ask of him, but I do believe he just might manage it.

"Shall we ask him his thoughts on the subject?"

"Let's do," smiled Ariel, as she raised her hand and signaled Tanis to join them.

He trotted over to them and dropped to one knee before her. "Relax, Tanis. Sit and tell us the tale of your success."

Smiling with delight he sank down a respectful distance from her. "We rode into the village, Lady, and the others held back, readying their bows. I approached the humans and told them I wanted the slaves brought out to me. I promised that, if they did as I asked, none would be harmed. I also promised that, in future Elves would trade fairly with them and all would prosper."

Mearith grinned. "I take it they refused your generous offer."

"They did," he laughed. "One threw a spear at me and another an arrow. The fight was on then, and they were soon defeated. We burned three huts to encourage them to hurry with the slaves.

"One slave told us there were more at a nearby farm, and with her to guide him to the place, Korath went to retrieve them. We then demanded traveling clothes for them all and refused to pay for them because they fought us."

Mearith smiled and lightly gripped his shoulder. "So, tell me, how did this adventure make you feel?"

He sighed and turned his gaze to the crackling fire as he spoke. "It was frightening, Lady, but not like you might think. I had no fear of the men and weapons I faced. It was my own rage that brought me fear. When they fought us, I wanted so badly to kill them all, to repay for all that was done to me and others before you rescued us."

"Tell me what held you in check, Tanis," Ariel said gently.

"I heard your voice, Lady, in my mind. You said to do that would make us no better than them. We can't undo what was done, the atrocities committed over the generations. All we can do is build a better future."

"And so, you stayed your hand," said Mearith. "Well done, Tanis. Yes, my delight, I do believe our young friend may just be ready."

Ariel smiled at his bemused look and patted his shoulder. "I have a mighty task for you when next we return to these forests in Spring, Tanis. When we do, we will divide into two major groups. I will lead one, you the other."

"Me? My queen?"

"Hush now, here's what I want to do. My group will focus on capturing another city and freeing all the slaves there. However, your group will make that a lot easier for me. Here's the plan.

"In early spring, we all, led by Mearith, will enter the mountains and establish two or more waystations. These waystations will be manned by Bornani for the most part, but they will have Borni warriors with them as well. Fugitive will also be such a place.

"Now, while I and mine are stalking a city of the Geni, you will lead a band of Elves, a hundred or more strong. You will strike at every farm, village, and small town you can find, take their slaves, burn them out. I want you to free as many slaves as possible and to fill Shotar with as many refugees as possible."

"Tanis, this will be the more dangerous task of all," said Mearith, "for your numbers will be smaller. Shotar will send hardened warriors against you. Do not fight them in open battle. Instead lure them into the forests, lead them astray, then circle behind them and strike at the villages again."

"This is a most dangerous mission, Tanis," said Ariel. "Will you take this on for me?"

"Gladly, my queen, if you believe this is a task I can manage, but would its success not be more assured if Lady Mearith or Arlon were to lead it?"

"I need Mearith with me to keep me grounded, Tanis. When in Elanda, I gained access to far too much power. That, as we know all too well, is the path to destruction. Lady Mearith is the only one who can hold me to the true path.

"Arlon is a fine general, and I trust him, but he has never felt the sting of the lash, nor has he endured the horror of a slave's life. The Bornani will be far more willing to follow and obey one of their own, Tanis. You know this to be true."

He nodded thoughtfully for a moment. "So, I am to lead mostly Bornani?"

"Yes, but you will have a few seasoned Borni with you as well. You may choose whoever you like to join your party. Just tell us what you'll need."

He suddenly looked up at Ariel. "What I'll need? This is a test, isn't it? Lady Mearith has taught you too well, my queen."

They had a good laugh at that. "Well?"

Tanis thought for a moment. "All right, I'll need a mage, a healer, extra clothing and such for the newly freed, and Kern."

"Kern? Tanis, Kern's not a warrior."

"Nor do I expect that of him, my queen. Kern is the master of the horse. If we're to strike far and wide we'll need horses, not war horses like Grimm, but smaller, faster, horses, horses that can move easily in the forest, yet outrun the big horses our pursuers will be riding.

"We'll need weapons of course. If I can, Lady, I'd like the Borni of my party to be those who are with us in this camp. I've gotten to know several and I not only trust them, but I believe they will trust me to lead them. As you have demonstrated so often, those who follow must trust the leader completely."

"It shall be as you require, my friend," smiled Ariel. "Will you want the rest of the guard with you as well?"

"My queen, I can't leave you without a guard."

"I'll choose a new guard from the Bornani when we reach Elfhome. Bring Trelanth and Eline to me now."

He rose easily and trotted off. He was soon back with the two Elves she had requested. Ariel explained her plan for the following year and asked their opinion.

The woman who led the fifty Borni grinned. "So, Tanis, you want me and the rest to play in the forest with you?"

"Come on, Eline, you know you want to," he grinned.

Her laughter was sweet and rich. "Yes, I do. My queen, we'd be delighted to join the Bornani in their adventure."

"You understand, Tanis is to command, even as thought it was myself leading the mission."

"I've come to trust Tanis, Lady. There'll be no problem at all. Tanis, I assume the Bornani will be having all the fun and the poor forgotten Borni will be in a supporting role."

"The Bornani will free the slaves, you'll have to make sure we don't get ourselves killed while we do it."

Her grin widened. "When do we start?"

"As soon as Trelanth assigns a mage to your party," said Ariel. "There's one more village in our path to Narthwood. Take your troops and clear that path."

"My queen," he said as he rose to his feet.

"Tanis, take Ethor with you. He's healed up and itching for some action," said Trelanth.

He grinned and trotted away, Eline right beside him. They watched as he stopped and spoke with Korath. Nodding, Korath sat back down while Tanis led twenty of the Borni plus Ethor into the night.

Ariel signaled for Korath who came to her instantly. "What did Tanis say to you?"

"He said to not leave you unguarded until we rejoin him on the path to Narthwood."

She shook her head and grinned. "That man will guard me whether I want him to or not."

Once again hooded riders approached a village at dawn. Several of the people gathered in the square as one rider approached. The headman leaned on his crutch and moved toward him. "Best of the morning to ye, stranger. What brings you and your company here?"

"I've come for your slaves," replied the hooded man. "Give them to me and nobody will get hurt. In future, Elves will come here to buy and trade fairly. In this manner, all will prosper."

"I see," grinned the headman. "And I suppose if I refuse you'll kill the lot of us and burn the village to the ground."

"You're a very perceptive man, sir," grinned Tanis as he pushed back his hood and dismounted. "That is indeed my intention. I have a score of warriors with me, more on the road behind, and if that's not enough to defeat so stout a folk, there are thousands just a few short days away. So, do we have a bargain?"

The man shifted his weight on the crutch then grinned. "Tell me, what if they don't want to go with you?"

"If that wish is sincere, they may choose their own fate."

"And who decides if the choice is made of free will?"

The man was still grinning and Tanis laughed. "The queen will decide," he replied. "She's on her way and will be here by high sun. When she comes, the Elves will be standing here will me, waiting for her. She will hear them and decide what is to be or not to be."

"So, you're just the messenger boy?"

Anger sprang to Tanis' eyes, but he fought it down. The man was trying to provoke him for some reason. Reason enough to deny him success. His smile widened. "Think of me more as a messenger with a peace offering.

"Actually, I have many tasks. I've delivered my message and now I set aside that task, for it's been completed. Now I move on the next task, retrieving Elves."

Tanis raised his arm high and thirty bows were drawn fully. Three others lit torches and moved closer to one of the huts. "Time's up, bring them to me now or I burn you out. Please say burn, for it's a cold day and I need to warm up."

The man gave a great roar of laughter then called out. "Garn, bring them out, our young friend is getting impatient." Tanis slowly lowered his arm as a door opened and six Elves followed an old man out into the cold air. These Elves seemed warmly dressed and healthy.

"All right," said the headman, "These are all the slaves in the village."

"What about the surrounding farms, are there any others there?"

The young boy Tanis had spoken to shook his head. "No, sir, everybody's here."

"So, what now, warrior?" asked the headman. For an answer, Tanis tossed him a bag of coins. "Ten gold for six slaves? You're a generous man, Warrior."

"You're content with the price then?"

"More than. So, what happens now?"

"Now we wait for the queen, then we leave. As I said before, in future we will come to trade from time to time. As long as you keep no slaves, we have no quarrel."

"And if I took this gold and bought a dozen slaves?"

"I'll come back and burn this village to the ground, with your corpse in it."

Once again that great bellow of laughter. "Then I'm fairly warned, Warrior. I'm Moll, headman of this now prosperous village."

"Tanis," he replied with a grin, as he offered his hand. "Moll, I've got to say, you're an easy fellow to deal with."

"Yes, well, my sister and her son arrived in the night. She told me what happened in her village, of how you killed most of the men and burned her out. I thought, if you came this way, that I might try something else." He tossed the bag of coins in his hand. "I'm quite pleased that I did."

Tanis turned to the slaves, drawing out his dagger as he did. "I must say, my brothers and sisters," he said as he deftly cut the collar from a man's neck, "you folk seem to be quite healthy. I take it Moll and friends feed you well."

"Since Master Moll brought us here eight years ago, we have been treated well, sir," replied the man. "We work hard, but so do all the masters. We're well fed and we have warm clothes to wear. Sir, can't we stay here?"

"You feel safe here?"

"Yes, Master. This is a good place."

"It's a better place where we're going. We're going to Elfhome, to join with the Borni there. In Elfhome there are teachers to help you learn things, food and clothing, other Elves, thousands of them, and no slaves. We each choose our own path in life. It will be the same for you, my friend."

"Truly this is so?" asked a young woman with a babe in her arms.

"It is," he replied, as he tickled the child and made her laugh. "Two years ago, I was a breed slave on my way to the auction block in Shotar. The queen came to us and set us free. The Borni taught us woodcraft and the use of weapons. I became the captain of the queen's guard, and so I am now."

"You chose this path of your own free will, Master?"

"Tanis, remember, just Tanis. Yes, I chose this. Actually, I told the queen she needed a guard and appointed myself to the post," he grinned. "Of the breed slaves in the group I was in, Beren has become the queen's healer, Belia was taken by the compulsion, and has mated with the king of the Borni, and the rest are in the queen's guard.

"You'll meet them soon."

"Tanis," said Moll. "Is there any truth to the tale the queen sacked the city of Magdan?"

"It's true, Moll. I was there. We brought out over a thousand slaves that day. Most of them are in Elfhome now. A few who were injured on the way will soon be here, escorted by the queen herself and her companion, Mearith the Merciless."

Moll rubbed his chin thoughtfully. "So, if you're headed to this Elfhome, and you came from the south, that must mean ..."

"Elfhome is in Narthwod forest. That I can tell you, but I'd prefer that be kept secret for now."

"You don't want the Geni to know. They'll find out, you know. Their magic will tell them that. They're probably watching us right now."

"You think so? Let's see. Ethor!"

One of the others approached. "Yes Tanis."

"Have the Geni been watching our adventures today?"

The newcomer laughed. "One did cast his eye over this area, but I showed him a peaceful village with downtrodden slaves laboring in the fields, and he moved on."

"Ethor, you're the best," grinned Tanis. "So, there you have it, Moll. No Geni watching."

"Now, since our new brothers and sisters seem fit to travel, perhaps we should move on. If we take our time the queen will catch up before dark."

"Before you go," said Moll, "there's just one more thing."

Tanis turned back to him with a raised eyebrow. "Oh?"

"Yes, you never did answer the girl's question. Are they allowed to stay here if they choose to do so? You did say something about the freedom to make their own decisions."

Tanis sighed and turned to the newly freed slaves. "I was just starting to like you, Moll.

"All right, my friends, please consider this. What will happen when the Geni tax collectors come looking for increased taxes, for come they will. It costs money to wage war, and the Geni will go to war against the queen. When the money is gone, which of you will be taken to pay the tax?

"I beg you, come with us, see Elfhome for yourselves, see what things are possible for you, and then, if you still wish to return here, do so. Just, come see the other possibilities for yourselves."

The woman who'd asked the question looked to Moll, confused. "Go with them, girl. See the place for yourself. The village will still be here when you get back."

Tanis gave him a long look. "Eline, take our new friends and head out. I'll await the queen and make my report. Find a campsite early and we'll catch up to you."

"At once, my Lord Tanis," she said with an impish grin. He shook a finger at her as she signaled the others.

Tanis tossed the woman with a baby up onto his horse. "You be careful now," he said to the horse. "You have a small passenger." The horse nudged him then set out at a walk.

The rest of the newly freed joined the march and they left the village.

Once the procession was well on the way, Tanis turned back to Moll. "I've got to say, Tanis, you're a bold one."

"Oh?"

"Sending all your warriors on ahead and staying behind by yourself."

Moll didn't even see the movement, but he suddenly felt the prick of the dagger at his throat. "I won't bother telling you all about the beatings, the torture, the humiliation, I've endured, nor will I bother with the tale of my mother's death because I fought the man who whipped her.

"Maybe I'll just tell you how badly I want your people to attack me so I can make someone pay for all that was done. Please, give the word." He stepped back and spread his arms wide to make himself an inviting target, a dagger in each hand.

"Nobody's going to attack you here, Tanis," Moll said gently. "I can't undo or take away what was done, but I can tell you this. That sort of thing has never been done here in Ramia."

"Oh?"

"I don't like slavery, Tanis, never did. I saw some cruelty when I was young, and I still hear the screams in my dreams. As soon as I could, I bought a few slaves, gathered a few friends of like mind, and we came here to establish a town.

"Those people you freed today were slaves in name only. They wore the collars only to keep suspicions down to a minimum. You were right though, if the tax collectors came and we couldn't pay they'd have taken our friends.

"I'll be honest with you, my young friend, once I learned the High Born Queen had arisen and was reclaiming her people I hoped she might pass this way. I expect they'll be safer with your folk in the long run."

Tanis dropped his stance and relaxed, shaking off the mood. "So, why did you put up such a fuss?"

"I was giving the people time to escape into the forest. Did you notice we're almost alone here?"

"I noticed, and I can tell you where each one went. Oh, I can't actually see them right now, but if I wanted to find them it would be all too easy. Besides that, they're returning now."

Moll looked up to see his people returning, being herded along by heavily armed Elves. "So I see. The woman on the big gray warhorse would be the queen, right?

"Well, I'm not sure if this old leg will bend far enough, but I'll give it a try." With that he stepped past Tanis to approach the queen.

Tanis dodged nimbly past him and knelt. "All is as required, Lady. Eline has gone on ahead with six new Bornani."

The queen leaned on the pommel of her saddle and grinned. "Rise, Tanis. So tell me, where's your horse?"

"Alas, my queen, she has left me here to carry another."

"That seems to happen to you a great deal. Perhaps you need a less fickle horse.

"So, who does she carry this time, an elder or an infirm?"

"A young mother with babe in arms, Lady," grinned Tanis.

Ariel smiled and nodded. "All is well here, my friend?"

"All is well, Lady. Moll here is the headman for this village, called Ramia. The man is a savage bargainer, Lady. We'll have to find important jobs for these newly freed, for he has emptied my purse."

Ariel laughed and dismounted. "No, stand, Moll. I can see your leg doesn't like to bend. So, you drive a hard bargain, do you?"

"I had no choice, Lady. The young savage was impoverishing my village. Why, now even I will have to take up a hoe and work at the fields."

"Somehow I get the impression you do that anyway. Tell me of it, friend of the Elves."

"I dislike slavery, Lady. As a child, I was punished for trying to protect the farm slaves. When I grew to manhood I saved my coin until I could buy a few slaves of my own. I then gathered some friends of like mind and came here. Here, the Elves were slaves in name alone, for we worked beside them, shared our homes, clothed and fed them as best we could.

"In truth, I'm glad you came for them, for now they're out of reach of the Geni."

"And they will remain so, friend Moll. Tanis paid you well?"

"He paid us well, Your Majesty. The folk of Ramia have lost only a few friends this day. They left with their own clothing, tools, and weapons. All they left behind was the oshar. Perhaps there's room in the wagon for a couple of barrels."

"Why would I want that?"

"Lady, what else are they going to eat?"

"You don't know, do you?" she asked, as she stepped closer. "No, I can see the concern for your friends in your eyes. Friend Moll, the oshar isn't a food, it's a poison. It dulls their Elvish senses and shortens their lives."

"But the madness..."

"No, Moll, without the oshar they won't go mad, they will awaken, even as I did, as Tanis has done. Fear not for your friends. Perhaps one day they may return to visit and tell you of their adventures."

"You're speaking the truth, aren't you," he said, his shoulders slumping. "Damnit, if we'd known we could have ..."

"Don't beat yourself up, my friend," smiled Ariel. "You did your best for them, and I thank you for it. From time to time in future you will have a visit from the Elves, to make certain all is well with you. Should disaster befall this village, head north into Narthwood. The Elves will find you there and take you to safety."

"Thank you, great queen. I must caution you, however, that secret location should be well guarded, for if the Geni should discover ..."

He took an involuntary step back from the wolfish snarl that came to her lips. "Let them come, I have no fear of the Geni. Come Tanis, lead us to our people, the day is growing old."

"My Lady." With a grin, he leaped to his feet and trotted out of the village. Ariel and the rest followed.

Narthwood

Two days later, they moved out onto the plain that separated Narthwood from the rest of the world. Tanis rode beside the queen and her companion.

"Mearith, my heart, this land formation is passing strange to me. Can you tell me how it came to be and why nothing grows here, why it lies barren, like a buffer between Narthwood and the rest of the world?"

"I can't say with absolute certainty, my delight. Before the world was broken this wasn't here, but a broad river flowed along this path. Perhaps your new senses can give us more information."

With a nod of agreement, Ariel closed her hand around the jewel that rode at her breast. Mearith steadied her in the saddle as her eyes focused far away.

Ariel watched as a wave of vile looking mist raced along the shining river, causing it to boil up. Suddenly a wave of crystal clear water came racing along to drown the mist, then the earth below the river bed bucked and heaved up, broke open.

The waters of the river drained into the hole in the earth then another wave of mist, a blue, calming mist came and sealed the rift. That mist swept out and flowed along the now dry riverbed. The riverbed rose up then settled, its surface flat and calm.

A tall mage stepped from the trees and spoke in a clear ringing voice. "From this moment forth you shall lie as a barrier, barren and broken. And here I lie with you, for I have spent my life force to seal this rift." Ariel watched as his body seemed to dissolve and spread itself out over the dry riverbed.

The vision faded and she returned to herself. She spoke to her companions of what she had seen.

Mearith nodded sagely as she described the mage. "Tomlin. So that's what happened to him. He was Onlay's younger brother, a powerful mage in his own right. When the Geni cracked open the world he must have stopped it here, preventing the world's complete destruction."

"I believe you're right, my heart," said Ariel, a gentle smile on her lips, "for I feel this place welcomes me. May your spirit be at peace, Tomlin, for we have returned, we survive, and we return to the forest once again. We thank you for guarding this place of passage."

They crossed that plain in a single day, although hunters and trappers all agree that it takes two. As they reached the first line of trees, Arlon stepped out and knelt. "Greetings, my queen, I hope your journey was uneventful."

"There was nothing we couldn't handle, my friend," smiled Ariel. "You arrived without mishap?"

"We did, Lady. My queen, I fear you will have to abandon your wagon, the forest is too dense for it to manage."

"And the horses?"

"They'll be fine," he smiled. Turning his head, he called out over his shoulder. "Kern, bring them out."

Ariel shrieked with delight as a lone rider burst from the forest followed by dozens of horses. Grinning, he rode up to the queen and inclined his head. "My queen."

"Kern, you seem to be enjoying yourself."

"I am, Lady. Before you came, I could not have imagined a life with such joy. Tell me how I can serve."

"Arlon informs me we must abandon the wagon. I believe all can ride, but most have no experience. We'll also need horses to carry packs.

Kern, are we going to be able to keep all these horses through the winter?"

"Yes, my queen. Near Elfhome lies a wide flood plain. It's mostly grassland and the wind will keep the snows from getting too deep. We will be able to graze them through the longest winter."

"Tell me, my young friend, just how did you come by this knowledge?"

"The horses told me, Lady. Several of those you see here are from a herd that runs wild on that flood plain."

Ariel laughed with delight. "Just how did you convince them to join you here?"

"I asked them, Lady. They were surprised that my Doana could run as fast as they could. They wanted to know all about us. Lady, they are quite remarkable horses."

"Oh?"

"Yes, they're as at home in the forest as they are on the open grasslands."

"Are they now?" said Mearith. "Kern, once we get these folks to Elfhome, I suspect Tanis will want to have a long talk with you."

"Oh?"

"Yes, my friend," grinned Tanis. "Our lady queen has given me a mighty task, and I'll need your help if I'm to succeed. Come, let's get these folks out of that wagon and onto a horse, then I'll tell you all about it. If your new horse friends are willing to help it'll make all our lives a lot easier."

Ariel and Mearith watched as Kern chose the horses for the inexperienced riders and Tanis helped them up. The experienced riders got more spirited mounts. In short order, they were on the move again.

As Narthwood swallowed them up, the trails seemed to magically appear. Daylight was fading when a camp of Bornani appeared in a forest glade, fires blazing cheerily, food cooking, and graze for the horses. The travelers dismounted and their horses were taken, rubbed down, and given a treat while the Elves were fed.

Each day saw a repeat of the same. A camp appeared at dusk, the fires glowing, food cooking, and people to tend the horses. There were a few snow flurries, but for the most part the weather cooperated, and the travel was fairly easy for a moon cycle.

Finally, they reached Kern's flood plain. Snow lay on the ground, but plenty of dried grasses stuck up through. A day to cross that then they reached the hills that rose high above it. Evanseth and Belia were waiting for them.

"Evan," shouted Mearith, as she leaped from her horse and embraced him as Ariel embraced Belia. They switched, then Evanseth stepped back, a smile of delight on his face.

"My queen, I'm so pleased you've finally arrived. We were starting to worry."

"All is well, Evan," smiled Ariel. "The forest seems quite welcoming. I was expecting a somewhat colder reception."

"She has awakened from her long slumber and welcomed us home. When we began to build temporary homes, she awakened. Ariel, this ancient forest is full of magic and love of Elves. Come, you must see what we've managed in just one season."

They mounted and led the way. Ariel laughed with delight several times as she was shown village after village with the homes woven from living trees. They were designed so a very small fire would easily cast enough heat to warm the occupants and cook their food.

At last they came to a hillside which held a large cavern. Inside that cavern the royal palace had been established as it had been in ancient times. "The forest showed this to us," said Evanseth, as he led them inside. "I believe this was the royal seat when Elves lived here before. The forest fairly sang with joy when we began to set up.

"It'll take us years and more to make everything complete, but I'm quite pleased with all we've managed to do in so short a time. The long tunnel there leads out through the other side of the hill, an escape route should we ever need one.

"I confess, once we can devote some time to it, I want to move the royal court out under the sky once again, but for now this will serve."

"Don't be too hasty, my new brother," smiled Ariel, as she gazed all around in wonder. "I'm sure our ancestors chose this location for good reason. It's well protected from the elements of winter. Perhaps a summer home in the trees above and this for the cold seasons would suit you better."

"Me? Ariel, you're the queen, this is your palace, such as it is."

Ariel smiled and hugged him gently. "No, Evan, this is your palace, my home is in Fugitive, and I plan to return there in spring. Come. Let's relax and rest for a time, then we'll spend the winter at plots and plans."

And so they did. Over the winter, she visited and spent time with each and every village. Ariel expressed her delight at finding the Bornani hard at work beside the Borni, learning the ins and outs of building homes, ways to coax plants to grow even in winter, and so much more.

Forges had been built and the smiths were hard at work as well, all with newly freed slaves eager to learn. The Bornani were no strangers to hard work, to the delight of their Borni teachers.

Runners of the forest were constantly out in the surrounding areas, hunting for food supplies, finding the most likely routes for escape if it became necessary, as well as keeping watch.

A small troop was ever on watch at the barren plain leading to the vast forest. From time to time, Tanis led a number of his people on that task. He had gathered a hundred volunteers, a group of equal numbers of Borni and Bornani. They set up their own camp and moved it often. Tanis was preparing them for the task to come.

He named the group the Queen's Reavers, and they all were now riding Kern's new horses. They practiced archery from horseback as well as all combat techniques the Borni could teach.

While Tanis prepared his troops, Ariel gathered volunteers for her waystations. She needed hunter-gatherers as well as smiths, weavers, farmers, and warriors. She had no trouble finding people eager to help.

Winter lingered in the north, but they knew the snows would be nearly gone back in Fugitive. On a bright, sunny, spring day they set out, nearly two thousand strong. With no wounded to hinder their speed, they traveled fast. Within a moon cycle they were past Shotar and high into the mountains.

They had to slog through some deep snows still in the mountain passes, but they reached a broad river valley known to Mearith. There they began to set up the first waystation. There was a small clan of Dwarves nearby and the trading soon began, first with news and stories, and then for goods and services. The Elvish healers were welcome, as were the Dwarven axes and hammers.

Ariel stayed two weeks with them, then set out with her warriors along the river valley. Eight days' travel and one mountain pass later, they were in another broad valley filled with a lush forest. Waystation number two was soon established, then she set out for Fugitive.

War Party

While the queen took her people into the mountains, Tanis kept to the lowlands. To those who lived close to the city of Shotar, it was a shock when over a hundred mounted Elves sped along the highway in the moonlight. News of that passage soon reached the ear of the king, but by then the Elves were once again in the forest.

They sat around small campfires, alive with anticipation for the coming adventure. The Bornani were eager to repay their former masters in kind, but the Borni helped them stay focused.

Tanis rose and spoke to the entire camp, his voice magically enhanced by Ethor. "My friends, hear me well. Like you, I have a burning desire to strike back at the masters, to repay for all that was done. We can't do that, brothers and sisters. We can't undo what was done, no matter how many we torture and kill.

"No, we must put that aside or become like them. Hear me, my brothers and sisters, we are not like them, we're better than that. We have a two-fold purpose, given us by the queen herself. First and foremost, we're here to set free all those Elves we can find. Our second purpose is to overload Shotar with refugees.

"Consider this carefully. Every Human, Orc, Dwarf, or Geni we leave alive will be a drain on Shotar's resources. Each one we kill can no longer serve our purpose. We must keep as many alive as possible.

"Having said that, we must impoverish them, take their slaves and horses, burn their homes and farms, so they'll have no other recourse except to flee to their king in Shotar.

"This is the reasoning as given me by Queen Ariel and Lady Mearith. When Shotar can hold no more refugees they will be sent away to starve or worse. That's when we befriend them, find them places of safety and more.

"Eventually they will turn against the Geni and become our allies. They will help us drive the Geni back to their barren lands to the south. This is our mission, this is why we're here, not for revenge.

"My brothers and sisters, I chose each and every one of you personally because I believe you're the people who can help me succeed in this. It's your task to make me look good in the eyes of the queen." This brought a round of laughter.

"Rest well this night, my friends. Tomorrow we go to war, tomorrow we strike the first blow." With that he sat down and sighed. They'd spent the winter preparing for this, the wait was over. Ready or not, it would begin with the rising of the sun.

"You're nervous," smiled Eline.

"Yes, I am. How did I get here? I mean, a few years ago, I was a breed slave bound for auction at Shotar. How did I end up here? What madness made Queen Ariel make me the leader of this war party?"

She laughed and gave him a friendly punch on the arm. "Listen, my young friend, you got here through proven ability. Some people are natural leaders, some of us learn those skills over time, and still others never do. Tanis, you're a natural leader, just like Queen Ariel herself, you inspire those who follow you. You were born with that, it's as natural to you as breathing.

"Me, I learned leadership over time, worked my way up to a command of fifty. No, my friend, I've watched you carefully from the day we met, trying to see how you managed to inspire folk so easily.

"You appointed yourself Captain of the Queen's Guard and she kept you in that role. Lady Ariel could have her choice of people from all the Borni, yet she left you in that role.

"Why? Because she could see you're a natural leader, a savage fighter, and utterly loyal to her. You're also the man with the keenest insights to any situation, and you're able to make good decisions in a heartbeat.

"Above and beyond that, as one of the first Bornani, these folk will trust and obey you more easily than a Borni. If a Borni were in command the Bornani might hold back, expecting the more experienced warriors to get the job done. With one of their own in command they're eager to get to it themselves."

Tanis blushed slightly under her praise. "Thanks, Eline. I suppose your warriors all believe the same reasoning."

"They do, and they're your warriors now, Tanis. We all willingly serve the queen and she's chosen you to lead us. We all agree her choice was a good one.

"Tanis, we're all more experienced, yes, but this is a new and different war we're fighting. You understand what we're up against, we don't, not to the same level. Trust yourself, my young friend, as we do." She patted his knee as she rose to her feet. "Get some rest." With that she walked away to take her turn at watch.

He did manage some sleep, but by the time the night began to lighten into day he was on his feet preparing his horse. The Elvish saddles were light and many of the horses wore none at all. These wild northern ponies were fierce creatures and more than willing to help their riders.

As the sun broke over the distant mountains, they sat waiting just within the trees. "Kern, are you ready?"

"Ready, my Lord Tanis," grinned Kern. "The campsite's ready, extra supplies are ready, and the horses are ready. They want us to bring out the horses, too."

"And we will. Eline, ready?"

"We're ready, my Lord Tanis. Are you sure about this?"

"Let's do it. Ethor, hide us now."

"Already done, my Lord Tanis."

"Let's go!"

With that Tanis urged his horse forward. They raced from the trees and down the hill into a large village that was just starting to wake up for the day. The Elves fanned out to surround every building while Tanis rode to the center of the square and shouted.

"Come out, people. Come out."

Bewildered they came, sleepy and blinking in the morning sun. "Who are you? What do you want here? This village is under the protection of the king. State your business." The speaker was an Orc with a battle axe across his shoulder.

"My name is Tanis. I've come to relieve you of your slaves. Bring them out, quickly now, before I lose patience with you."

"Get off that horse and I'll show you patience," snarled the Orc, slipping his axe to the ready position.

"As you wish," replied Tanis, as he leaped nimbly from the saddle.

With sword in hand he charged. The Orc was startled at his speed and barely managed to parry the first thrust. The axe missed on the back swing, but the sword didn't.

Tanis kicked the Orc's falling body off his blade and shouted. "Bring out those slaves, all of them, or I'll gut every living creature, man, woman, beast, or child, in this village, and then burn it to the ground. Quickly now."

When no one moved, he signaled with one hand and a man fell, clutching the arrow protruding from his shoulder. "Move it." They began to move. Soon the square was full of slaves.

Tanis gave a shrill whistle and a dozen riders came forward with extra horses. Soon all the slaves were on horseback and leaving the village for the forest beyond. Tanis turned back to the village folk. "Come out of your homes, now. Eline, loot every hut then burn it. Bort, gather up what horses you can find and get them into the forest."

At his command, several Elves began searching and looting the houses and barns. The horses were kept, money and other things of value were kept, and then the huts were set afire. All the while hard-eyed archers watched the gathered villagers carefully.

Three more slaves were found and spirited away, then Tanis turned and pointed to the spires of Shotar in the distance. "Hear me people, go there to that city, and tell your king that Tanis of the Bornani will send him more loyal subjects soon. Go, or I'll start killing until you move."

As one, the terrified villagers fled toward Shotar. Once they were well away, the rest of the buildings were set afire. Tanis and companions mounted and disappeared into the trees.

Tanis smiled as they reached the site of the previous night's camp. The slaves were now all free of the collars and were standing together, bewildered. He hopped down from his horse to speak to them. "Kern, are we all good here?"

"Yes, my Lord Tanis. All our new friends can ride to one degree or another. Three are injured and one ill, but Garin is seeing to their hurts."

Tanis nodded. "Garin, is it safe for them to travel?"

"It is, my Lord."

Again he nodded. "Eline."

"Yes, my Lord?"

"What is all this my lord stuff about? It's starting to get irritating."

"You lead a hundred, my Lord," she grinned. "Once long ago, when the Elves were as the leaves in the forest, one had to rise to lead a thousand before earning the title of Lord Commander. However, with our numbers as they are, we who run with you have decided a hundred should earn the title in the world as it is now.

"Tanis, the Bornani know you as one of their own, by wearing the title you become one of the Borni as well. This will reinforce your leadership with your Borni warriors. Don't refuse it out of hand."

He nodded thoughtfully then turned to the newly freed slaves and spoke in the common language. "My brothers and sisters, I'm sure that Kern has told you what's going on. Your collars are gone forever. I can see you're as confused by this event as I was when Queen Ariel set me free. You have questions, but I beg you to save them until tonight.

"By now I'm certain someone in Shotar has spotted the refugees. Soon troops will be dispatched to recapture you. I'd rather that didn't happen. We'll go deeper into the forest to a place we know. There we will spend the night, and I'll do my best to answer all your questions there.

"So, have you been given food?"

"Yes, Master," said one man, bowing his head. "We were given food and water, but there was no oshar. Sir, we need oshar or we'll die."

"No, my brother," smiled Tanis. "I won't let you die. Let's all mount up now and be on our way. We'll take care of you when we stop for the night.

"Ethor."

"My Lord?"

"Let the Geni see the village now, but keep prying eyes off us." The mage grinned and set to work.

"Kern, take these folks to the camp we agreed upon, the rest of us will make certain we're not followed."

All through the day the nimble little ponies trotted through the trees, down forest paths, scrambled up steep hills, crossed streams and more. Finally, as the sun began to sink below the mountains in the distance, they reached a clearing where three Elves had fires going and food cooking.

Tired, they slid wearily to the ground, but Kern stopped them. "Wait, good people. These beautiful beasts have carried you safely throughout the day. Now it's time to thank them for their help. I'll show you how to strip off the saddles and rub them down, and then we'll eat and rest."

They watched him carefully as he demonstrated how to care for the horses, listening to him talk to them, as well as give instruction. Hesitantly at first, they began to help rub down the horses and talk to them. Tanis grinned to see many of the newly freed suddenly smile as a weary horse turned to give a friendly nuzzle as a thank you.

Once the horses were tended everyone settled down to eat and rest. Tanis grinned at the confused looks on the newly freed faces. "I can see it's time for those questions, my new friends. Ask what you will, and I'll try to make it clear to you what's going on."

"Lord Tanis, what's to become of us?" asked one woman fearfully.

"Let me tell you a story, my new sister. A few years ago, I was a breed slave on my way to auction. Queen Ariel came and set me free. She and her lady companion helped me through the awakening, to become a true Elf. She then gave me free choice about what would happen to me, the direction my life would take.

"I want the same for you, my brothers and sisters. Many of these people who brought you to freedom this day were once slaves as you were. Queen Ariel freed them just as we have freed you. I want to take you to a place of safety where you will be able to make these decisions for yourselves, a place where you can live free."

"Is there truly such a place, my Lord?" asked another.

"There are several," he smiled in reply. "The first is Fugitive." They gasped and began to look at each other hopefully. "Yes, my friends, Fugitive does exist. In that place, Elves, Orcs, Humans, and Dwarves live and work together in harmony. We want to take you there."

"But, what about the oshar, my Lord? Won't we all be dead of the madness long before we reach that place?"

"No, my brothers and sisters, you won't die or go mad. The oshar isn't a food to keep us alive, it's a poison to dull our senses and shorten our lives. Once off the oshar, you don't go mad, you awaken to all your Elvish senses. Many of these people sharing food with you now have experienced this."

The newly freed looked about furtively, but all they saw was smiling faces and several nods of agreement. "My Lord Tanis," said a young woman, "you say we will be able to choose our own path in life. Can you tell us what that means?"

He smiled to reassure her. "Perhaps you've heard that last year the queen captured the city of Magdan and freed all the slaves." Several of them nodded so he went on.

"Some of those people are here with you now. Others chose to remain in Elfhome, to study healing, building, smithing, or any number of other things. Still others are traveling with Queen Ariel, setting up waystations, places of rest and refuge for the newly freed people like you on their way to Elfhome."

As they mulled that over Eline stood to address them. "Brothers and sisters, there is one other thing you should know. We Elves, all of us, serve the queen. In this group, Lord Tanis represents her. We serve him and obey his every command without question. We must ask the same of you."

"So we're still slaves," came a soft mutter.

"No," replied Eline, "not at all. To serve the queen or one of her commanders is not slavery, for we all choose to do it of our own free will. Let me tell you something of Lord Tanis. He may command me into danger, but he will always be there in as much or greater danger, for he won't ask me to do what he would not.

"Queen Ariel is the same. They do not ask you for personal service, for you saw Lord Tanis unsaddle and rub down his own horse, carry his own food and more. We serve because we are honored to do so.

"Before we can take you to Fugitive or on to Elfhome, you must swear loyalty to the queen as represented here by Lord Tanis. If you choose not to become one of us then you may go where you will, we won't try to stop you."

As they considered that Tanis rose to his feet and pulled off his tunic, exposing his badly scarred back for all to see. As they gazed in wonder another man rose and revealed his scars too. Soon all the Bornani had exposed their scars.

"As you can see," said Tanis, "we've all been where you are, facing that same decision. We are the Bornani, the Children of the Forest." He suddenly grinned. "Join us, brothers and sisters, come on, you know you want to."

One of the women rose to her feet and approached him. She pointed at one of the Bornani, a woman. "I know that woman," she said. "I've seen some of the abuse she suffered when we were younger. She looks so strong now, so free and at ease, so happy. I want to be like her. I promise I'll obey every command you give. Just teach me to be like her."

"We will do that and more," said Tanis. "So, how about the rest of you? Join with us and be loyal subjects of the queen?"

There was a slow round of agreement. Most of them were still afraid, but the glimmers of hope were starting to be seen in their eyes. "Excellent," smiled Tanis. "Eline, these folks could use some better clothing, and perhaps a personal guide for the journey to Fugitive."

"As you desire, My Lord, so shall it be." He sighed and shook a finger at her, but she laughed and danced away, calling for the supplies. Soon all the former slaves were dressed in warm clothes and snuggled into new cloaks. There were plenty of smiles and hopeful hushed conversations as the camp settled down to sleep.

The next morning Tanis was building up the fire and chatting with Eline as three scouts came into camp. They approached and knelt, "My Lord Tanis."

"Don't do that, my friend. Never kneel to me, kneel to the queen, but never me. We're comrades in arms, friends, nothing more." He switched to the common language so the newly freed could understand. "Let me be clear, my people, you kneel to the queen and her consort, not to me."

"But my Lord Tanis," grinned Eline. "In this place and time, you ..."

"No, not this, I won't have it."

"Tanis?"

"I was forced to kneel to receive the whip, as were many of these others."

She smiled gently. "My Lord, you hold no whip, nor do we fear your displeasure. It's a sign of love and respect. Will you not accept it from us?"

He looked thoughtful for a moment. "I know you Borni are a bunch of traditionalists, and I love that about you. So, how about this, save the kneeling for the true royals. Give me this salute instead." Grinning he lightly slapped his left fist against his right shoulder.

The Borni warriors all looked at each other for a moment then Eline grinned and nodded. As one they stood and gave the salute. "Hail Lord Tanis!" the Bornani stood and repeated the salute as did the newly freed slaves.

Tanis blushed and grinned. "Hail and well met, Queen's Reavers. Now, what news of our back trail?"

"It's clear, my Lord," replied one of the scouts. "A hundred warriors, mostly Orcs, rode out from Shotar. They followed our trail into the forest, but quickly lost their way. Their horses were too big to carry armored riders through the paths we traveled. They gave up long before nightfall. They camped in the burned-out village, and then set out for Shotar at first light.

"One man, a tracker, remained behind and took up the trail."

"And his fate?"

"An arrow from the trees, my Lord. Even if a Geni was watching, nothing was revealed, and he progressed no farther than the riders did yesterday."

"Good news indeed. We'll take our time today then cross the king's highway in the night. With luck, we can make Fugitive in half a moon cycle."

They broke camp and moved out. Some watched the back trail, others scouted ahead, and each newly freed slave had a Bornani riding beside them. Finally, one man, struggling a bit to remain in the saddle, came alongside Tanis.

He bowed his head deferentially. "My Lord, may I speak?"

"What's on your mind, my brother?"

"It's that man, Kern. He's lame."

"That's true. This bothers you?"

"No, my Lord. It's just that, once on a horse, he changes. He's not even using a saddle or bridle. He talks to the horse, and, well, you said we could choose how we live our lives, and ..."

"You want to work with the horses?"

"Yes, my Lord. I'd never ridden before yesterday, and I know I have so much to learn. Do you think Kern would teach me? It's amazing a crippled man has lived so long, let alone become a man of importance."

"Let's ask him," grinned Tanis. He raised his arm and signaled for Kern.

With a grace of movement that was amazing to watch the horse easily changed course and approached. "Yes, my Lord?"

"Kern, you'll be needing help with all the horses. This worthy fellow wants to learn to be a horse guardian, like you. Will you tell him how you came to be as you are, and will you teach him?"

"Gladly, my Lord Tanis. My friend, I was one of those Queen Ariel brought out of Magdan. The Borni were so kind to me, something I had never known before. I could see my infirmity was holding the others back and so I asked the queen to kill me so they might travel faster."

Here he got a wistful smile on his face. "She refused and named me Kern after the lame horseman of legend. She charged me to learn all I could of horses, and Lord Tanis brought me this delightful creature that carries me. From that day to this, I have tried to learn more of horses, and how to help them.

"Come on, my new brother, we'll start with how to stay in the saddle. You're working too hard at it. Relax your body, lean forward a bit, and let her rhythm carry you."

Tanis winked at Kern and rode on ahead. "What think you, Ethor?" he asked, as he pulled alongside the mage.

Ethor grinned in response. "I think the Geni mages are somewhat perplexed, my Lord. They seem to be searching for something, or someone, but it eludes them. It must be difficult for them to concentrate with all those people shouting at them to find it."

Tanis laughed with delight. "That's good news indeed. So, tell me, what happens when you sleep, for you've not slept since before we struck the village."

"Not to worry, they're searching in the wrong place. Once we're across the highway, we'll be well out of the search area, and I'll ward the camp carefully before I rest."

"Then all is well." Tanis gave his shoulder a friendly pat and rode ahead to Eline.

"All is well, my Lord?"

"I believe it is, Eline. How are we doing?"

"Actually, we're doing better than I'd hoped. In honesty, I doubted your decision to go on horseback, believing we could make better time and more easily elude pursuit while on foot. These wonderful ponies Kern brought us are amazing in the trees."

"I know. We're traveling down trails Lady Ariel's Grimm would never be able to manage, the same for Lady Mearith's charger."

"Yes, but they will need their war horses, for they fight a far different battle than we do. Tanis, my friend, I sense you're troubled. What is it?"

"What we did, Eline, what we must do over and over again. I had no problem killing the Orc, nor facing anyone else in battle. It was the screams of terror from the women and children. You've never had to hear that, as I have. It tears the heart from me every time."

"Tanis?"

"I was a slave, Eline. I grew up with those sounds ringing in my ears, the cries of the innocent and helpless."

"You'll get used to it; you'll have to."

"And that's the part that frightens me, for I don't want to become like the slave owners."

"You won't, I won't let you. Tanis, compassion for the enemy, especially in battle, is deadly, you dare not allow it. Once the battle is over then that's another matter. Yes, we terrorized those people, but we didn't harm them, and they'll be safe within the city.

"If the queen's plan runs true, and we must believe it will, then one day we'll get to make some amends. I understand people, Tanis, and I'm sure there were plenty of cruel masters who enjoyed abusing their slaves. I'm equally as certain there were some who were kind to the slaves. Moll for instance. He can't have been the only one.

"The real problem here, my friend, is tradition."

"Tradition?"

"Yes. These folk were born and raised with slaves; they know of no other way to live. That's what we're doing, teaching them another way, a more self-reliant way to live.

"We remove the slaves and force them to see Elves as equal beings, beings capable of fighting back, refusing to do the work for nothing, refusing to accept the abuse. Once they learn to see us in a different light, then we can build a new way of living, with all peoples as equals.

"That was the mistake of the Borni long ago. We tried to push the others back, keep them out. We fought them instead of working with them; had we tried perhaps we could have found a better way. Had we done that we could have united, the Dwarves, the Humans, the few Orc clans, the Borni and the High Born, to block the Geni forces and drive them back."

"Do you think that could have been possible?"

"I'd like to think so. Our chances would have been better at any rate. However, that's not what happened, and so, here we are. It now falls to us to help Lady Ariel create the new world she's envisioned. That's why we're doing what we are, Tanis my friend. That's why we do what we do, as hard as it is."

He nodded thoughtfully then sighed. "Thank you for that, Eline. You've given me a new perspective, and eased my mind. What would I do without you?"

"Oh, you'd be completely lost, there's no doubt at all." That brought a great bellow of laughter from him, and he playfully took a swipe at her. She laughed as she leaned out of reach.

"So, you've dealt with unseasoned warriors before, have you?"

"We all go there from time to time," she smiled in reply. "We all do. The key is to have someone you trust to talk to, to help you through it."

"Thank you, Eline. Keep an eye on me?"

"I will, my Lord Tanis, I will. Look, that's the cliff up ahead. Isn't that where you want to cross the highway?"

"Yes. From there it's a straight run to Fugitive. We'll have to keep an eye out for pigmen, but with these horses we can move quickly. The main thing will be to make sure we leave no trail for someone to follow."

"Leave that to me and my people. We'll make sure no one follows."

They stopped to rest and eat a cold meal while they waited for darkness to enfold the world. It was a desolate section of the highway and there were no eyes to see as the two hundred Elves crossed and vanished into the forest on the other side.

"Eline."

"Yes, my Lord Tanis?"

"We have forty new Bornani. Choose fifty to guide and protect them. They can deliver them to Fugitive then rejoin us."

"Tanis?"

"It'll take a moon cycle to get there and back. I don't want to take that long to hit them again."

"Agreed."

She swiftly set about the task. Soon she returned to him with a tall Elf in tow. "I thought Dellan should lead them."

"Good choice," smiled Tanis. "Dellan, you're our best tracker. Be gentle with them, but get them to Fugitive, then return to us as quickly as possible."

"Yes, my Lord, and where will I find you?"

"Oh, I'm sure you'll be able to track us down." This brought a great laugh from the tracker. "Leave Kern and his new apprentice with me. Take who and whatever else you need."

"Yes, my Lord." At dawn, the folk bound for Fugitive set out. Half a moon cycle later they arrived. During the trip, they had gone through the awakening, learned a smattering of the old language, learned some woodcraft and weapons handling.

At Fugitive, they were welcomed and the Borni there took over their education. Dellan made a full report to L'ark, as well as to Marc and his advisers, then set out to find Tanis again. He found them right where he'd left them over three weeks past.

"Ho, Dellan, well met," grinned Tanis as Dellan and company stepped out of the trees.

"My Lord Tanis. You've been busy I see. How many new Bornani have you this time?"

"Forty-seven."

"So, am I returning to Fugitive again?"

"Yes. All went well with you?"

"We had a surprise from a group of pigmen. They managed to surprise us and killed two before we even knew they were there. Somehow, they were able to hide themselves from our eyes until battle was joined.

"Fugitive has a new smith called Freida, she's an Elf. She managed to make these amulets that we wear. If an unseen enemy is near the amulet will glow red and show the enemy to you. On the way back we had the opportunity to test them out. They work just fine. We'll lose no more people to the pigmen."

"That's good to know," said Eline. "I didn't know the pigmen had any magic."

"It appears to be something new," replied Dellan. "The new smith made a magic sword. It was finished on the day the pigmen attacked Fugitive in force, using the magic to cover their approach. Freida leaped over the wall, and, naked to the waist from working at the forge, killed half of them and drove the rest back into the forest.

"L'ark said she was a fearsome sight. After that battle one of the humans brought an amulet he'd taken from a dead porker. Her sword turned blue and so she made these for everybody to wear. I've brought a sack of them for the rest of you.

He smiled as he passed an amulet to Tanis then handed the bag of them to Eline. "I see you've been busy while I was gone."

"We were, that and more. Rest for the night, Dellan, then take these folks to Fugitive."

When Dellan set out the next morning, Tanis led his people in a new direction. Late that night he, Kern, Ethor, and Eline stood just inside the trees on a high bluff. "Well, there they are, just as I remember them."

Eline nodded as she gazed at the three villages in the moonlight. One was almost a town by size with a smaller one just a few miles on each side. They were about midway between Magdan and Shotar. "My Lord, why do I think you plan to hit all three at once?"

"You know me too well, Eline. Kern, advise me. I want to hit the main town first. A strike through the heart. We sweep down from the northeast, right through the main square then split up. We're about a hundred strong, but the two smaller villages could easily be taken by twenty.

"What I need to know is this, do we have enough horses, and are they fast enough to elude pursuit?"

"We do and they are, my Lord, but I suggest a different tactic."

"Oh? How would you do this?"

Shyly the lame horseman pointed to the east. "I'd come out of the rising sun into the first village. Enough warriors to take the community remain to free the slaves while the rest continue on to the next. Once the larger village is under control enough warriors continue on to the last.

"We burn them out, then let them see us moving into the forest there, as though we're heading toward Shotar. We then swing around to the east again, cross the highway in the night, then make for Fugitive."

Tanis nodded thoughtfully. "What say you, Eline?"

"I like Kern's plan, my Lord."

"As do I. Ethor?"

The man's gaze seemed far away. "The plan is sound, my Lord, but there's a problem."

"Oh?"

"There are more than a dozen heavily armed men in the town there. They appear to be soldiers, Human and Orc. Probably sent there to protect the town."

"Hmm, well forewarned is forearmed, as they say," mused Tanis. "Only a dozen or so?"

"Eighteen at most, but there are the townsmen to consider."

"What do you want to do, Tanis?" asked Eline.

"I want to take all three villages. Ethor, can you pinpoint which buildings house the soldiers?"

"They are all at the inn, my Lord."

"All right, then we hit them deep in the night. Eline, ready the fighters. We'll slip into the village and take them just before dawn. As soon as we have that under control you take twenty and go one way, send another twenty to go the other. Get some rest."

Deep in the night a hundred shadows left the forest and ran swiftly into the small town. They fanned out to cover every building, with most approaching the inn. At Tanis' signal torches were lit and hurled into the inn.

As the fire blazed up people came running out, shouting "Fire!" Most were trying to haul on clothes as well as help others out. The women and Elves were ignored, but every man or Orc with a weapon was brought down with arrows.

"It's an attack, we're under attack," bellowed a huge Orc as he tore an arrow from his shoulder. He swept his broadsword to the ready as Tanis moved in at alarming speed. The Orc's mail shirt deflected the dagger meant for his heart and he managed a glancing blow at the young Elf.

Tanis rolled back to his feet, ducked beneath the sword stroke, and delivered a crushing kick to the Orc's knee. As the huge warrior toppled sideways, Tanis drove his sword through the creature's neck. Pulling his sword free, he looked up to see several more dead fighters and a large group of terrified people.

"I want all the slaves and I want them now," he shouted, as he wiped his blade on the fallen Orc's body. "Hear me well, get those slaves here to me quickly or we'll start killing until there's no one left to kill. Bring them out."

"It's those damned Elves," said one man. He said no more as Tanis's dagger suddenly appeared in his chest.

"Start moving or I'll start killing. Bring me the Elves, all of them."

They were brought out, male, female, young and old, they came, frightened and trembling. There were nearly fifty of them. Each one was taken by an Elvish warrior and led out of the town. The rest of the small town's inhabitants were herded out in the general direction of Shotar.

As soon as the town was empty, every building was set afire. There was no looting, for there was no time. The refugees huddled in fear when mounted Elves raced past them as the dawn lightened the world. They soon saw the smoke of burning buildings from the nearby village.

By the time they arrived, the place was a burned-out ruin. The Elves could be seen taking the slaves into the forest and vanishing in the trees.

Once in the trees and out of sight Tanis called a halt. "Ethor, how did we do?"

"We have nearly seventy newly freed slaves, My Lord Tanis. We have three wounds, none serious, all can travel."

"Excellent. Kern, how are we off for horses?"

"We've enough, my Lord, but only just. If Eline brings out many more some of us will have to double up."

"Well then, shall we go see how she's doing?" He wheeled his horse and set out along a trail that couldn't be seen from the highway. The sun was well up when they met Eline's party.

"Eline, what news?"

"We were successful, my Lord. Twenty-three freed people, and no deaths on either side. We've gathered a few horses, and some supplies before we lit the torches."

"Good news indeed. With the horses Kern managed to round up from the battle in the town, we seem to be in good shape.

"All right, people, the time of battle has passed. We now make for Fugitive. We'll let the king's warriors scour the countryside looking for us while we take our new brothers and sisters to a safe haven. Everybody choose a companion and let's move out."

In the end, only three horses had to carry double, but as soon as Tanis gave up his horse to an old woman, two other Bornani relinquished their mounts as well. They ran easily beside the horses, smiling and chatting with the newly freed to ease their minds.

They were nearly in sight of Magdan before they crossed the highway and took to the forest again. Ethor made certain they passed unseen by prying eyes.

By this time, the newly freed were going through the awakening. The Bornani all smiled, enjoying the experience again with their new friends. Three days later, Dellan reached them. With the added help, they were able to travel faster. They arrived at Fugitive to find the queen and her thousand warriors waiting for them there.

Fugitive

The sun was high in the sky when a young Elf raced from the trees. "The queen," he shouted, as he neared the palisade of Fugitive. "The queen comes."

People poured out of the now fortified town to see over a thousand Elvish warriors emerge from the forest. At the head of the column rode Ariel astride the mighty Grimm with Mearith at her side.

As she neared them the people dropped to one knee. Laughing with delight, Ariel leaped nimbly from the saddle. "Rise good people, rise and greet me as a friend, for I've been too long away from home."

They rose to their feet and Drakkat caught her as she threw herself into his arms. She squealed with delight as he swung her about in the air. "Put her down, Drakkat," called Mearith, "you're killing her." Grinning, he set her on her feet and she grabbed Meg in a bear hug.

She was still greeting her friends, hugging each in turn when Mearith reached Drakkat. "I think somebody's happy to be home," he said.

"She is," replied Mearith, matching his grin and grasping his huge arm in the warrior's grip, "and so am I."

The reunion of old friends went on for the rest of the day before Ariel could set up court in the inn as in days past. She was just settling down to a bowl of stew and moaning her delight when L'ark entered, gently pulling a shy woman behind him. Mearith patted Ariel's arm to get her attention then pointed toward the door.

Ariel rose to her feet as L'ark approached with his companion. They both knelt. "Rise, L'ark and companion. L'ark, who is this woman with the shining sword and arms of a smith? I know her, I believe."

She stepped past him to inspect the woman more closely. This one was scarred badly, yet her arms rippled with hardened muscle. "Telee? By all the gods, it is you." Ariel grabbed the woman in a hug, speaking her name over and over again, tears of joy in her eyes.

"Ariel, by all the gods, you did it. You broke free and rescued me, just as you swore to do. You did it."

"Yes, and I swear I will keep you near me and keep you safe from now on. No one will ever raise a whip to you again."

To Ariel's surprise Telee loosed her arms around the Queen's shoulders. "If any try they will die by my hand," she replied with a fierce grin. "My name is Freida now. I work at the forge with Rolfin. Together we made this blade that cuts through armor as easily as through new fallen snow."

Ariel stepped back, a smile of delight on her face. Freida passed her the sword. The queen admired the weapon then returned it. "Come sit with us, meet Mearith, the delight of my heart, and tell us the tale of this weapon." She gently tugged Freida's hand and sat her at the table.

Ariel introduced Mearith, then Freida told the tale of her rescue and of how the Dwarves helped her find new joy and purpose in life. Marc told the tale of the attack on Fugitive and of how Freida had killed half of the attackers and driven off the rest.

"Freida," smiled Ariel. "It's a powerful name, for I've heard that tale, and you've earned it. So be it. I had hoped to make a warrior of you and take you with me, but it seems you're already a warrior to contend with."

"This is magnificent work," said Mearith, as she inspected Freida's sword. "My father had one in his private study. When the demon came, he wasn't able to reach it before he was killed, but the demon couldn't lift the sword, neither could the Geni who controlled him.

"I've been a warrior since long before the breaking of the world, and I've seen a few of these swords, but none finer." She passed it back. "Queen Ariel considers Fugitive her home, as do I. It pleases me this sword will remain here in the hands of a friend to defend it."

Freida smiled shyly as she returned the sword to the scabbard L'ark had made for it. Ariel stood and pulled Freida to her feet facing her. She crossed her wrists, palms facing Freida who suddenly grinned with delight and returned the gesture. They laced their fingers together and Ariel spoke.

"Ariel and Telee were fully pledged sisters. I, Queen Ariel, do now renew that pledge with my sister, Freida, Warrior of the Forge."

"And I, Freida of the Forge, do renew my vow of sisterhood and loyalty to my queen, Ariel."

"And so it is," said Ariel. "Ever were we sisters of the heart, and so we are still." She untangled their hands and hugged Freida again. "By all the gods, it's good to find you alive and whole, my sister. Look at you, so strong and fierce."

Freida laughed with delight, her shyness falling away at last. "And you, my sister, queen of all the world with thousands of Borni warriors to help you free the slaves. Ariel, I swear, I'm starting to believe we can do it. I mean, you will do it. I always knew it would be you to set us all free."

She started to kneel again, but Ariel stopped her. "No. Do not kneel, not you. Mearith doesn't kneel to me, Kern the lame horseman doesn't kneel to me, and my sister will not kneel, ever again. I can see by her scars she has done enough of that for a lifetime. Promise me now."

"As you wish, my queen, but you'll have to keep Drakkat from chopping off my head."

Ariel laughed heartily and shook a threatening finger at Drakkat who feigned a wide-eyed innocence. She returned to her seat then sighed. "Will no one speak to me of Randall? What has become of my friend and mentor? Has he passed into the mystery?"

"He has gone to live with his sister, to live out his remaining days with family, my queen," said Marc. "Sadly, the village they lived in was raided by Lord Tanis and the Queen's Reavers. They brought out nearly forty new Bornani, but ..."

"Randall?"

"Lady, we do not know of his fate. I'm sure that, had Tanis known he was there, he'd have brought him to us."

Ariel let her shoulders slump. "Yes, you're right, Marc."

"Marc, did I hear you call him Lord Tanis?" asked Mearith. "Has our young friend taken on airs then?"

"No, Lady Mearith," grinned L'ark. "It was Eline's idea, and I had to agree with her reasoning. There are so few of us now she felt to lead a hundred would be enough, and that the Borni in his party would be more comfortable with him wearing the title. In truth, it embarrasses him each time he hears it."

Mearith laughed at that then answered Ariel's unspoken question. "My delight, in the days when we Borni were many, one who led a thousand to war earned the title of Lord Commander. For the Borni to give Tanis this title speaks of trust and loyalty above and beyond the call of duty.

"Of those Borni who remain to us, only Arlon still holds the title."

"And you?"

"I'm of the royal house, my delight. It was not needed. For a man to wear that title will command respect and instance obedience from any of the Borni."

Ariel turned to Arlon. "You never mentioned this, but come to think of it, I recall hearing you addressed that way by some of the warriors. Tell me truly now, should I be using your title when I address you?"

"Nay, Lady, for if you do Drakkat will die of laughter, and we need him to lead his clan." There was a great round of laughter at that.

"Still," said Ariel, a twinkle in her eye. "I think Tanis should earn the title in the traditional manner. Mearith, my heart, was there some sort of ceremony involved in the bestowing of this title?"

"Actually, there was. The warrior would kneel before the king who would touch him on the shoulders with a sword and bestow the title upon him."

"I see. Well then, I believe there should be no shortcuts. Tanis will have to earn his title in the traditional manner. My Lord Arlon, prepare a thousand men. As soon as Tanis returns to us he can lead them on a raid, thus earning his title."

"With pleasure, my queen," grinned Arlon. "From what Marc tells us, he is well worthy of the name. Marc, what is the count?"

"We have nearly a hundred new Bornani with us and the runner who arrived yesterday says he's bringing nearly as many more. He should be here any day now."

Ariel smiled and nodded. A quick glance around the room showed her Olan sitting quietly near the door. She had greeted him warmly upon her arrival, but a sudden idea came to her. "Olan, will you join us?"

"Of course, my queen," he smiled, as he rose and crossed the room. Mearith nodded her approval, the man moved more like a warrior now instead of a farm slave. Obviously, he'd been training.

He sat and Ariel reached over to pat his arm. "So, my old comrade in arms, are you still determined to go to war?"

"I am, my queen. Lady, I want to help free those still in chains."

"And so you shall, my friend, so you shall. Recently I lost a member of my personal guard. I'd like you to join the Guard to bring their numbers back up. In this manner, you will once again protect my back in battle. Will you do this for me?"

"With great pleasure, my queen," he replied with obvious delight.

"Then so be it. Korath."

"My queen."

"Olan, Korath is now Captain of the Guard. Korath, Olan is the newest member of your troops. See that he has weapons and a horse worthy of his new post."

The young warrior grinned. "At once, my queen. Come, old friend, let's go see which of the horses wants to carry you to war with the queen."

Ariel smiled as she watched them leave. She then turned to Freida again. "Tell me of these invisible pigmen, my sister."

"I don't know much. We'd just finished making the sword and I was polishing it when it suddenly began to glow. There was a cry of alarm from the wall, and I ran toward it. The pigmen were there and I attacked them.

"Later we discovered their amulets that made them invisible until battle was joined. As soon as a blow is struck the magic is gone and all can see them. Rolfin and I made these small amulets in the same manner as the sword, for it takes both Dwarf and Elf smiths working together to make the metal. They turn red when and enemy is near and let you see him."

Trelanth leaned across the table and held her hand over Freida's small amulet. "This is well done, My Lady Princess." Freida was startled at the use of a royal title. "Is there any chance one of those amulets taken from the pigmen can be found?"

"Right here," said Marc. "We keep this one so Lady Freida can test the ones she makes before the warriors trust their lives to them."

He passed it to Trelanth who held it in her hand for a moment then dropped it to the table with a snarl. "That is a truly vile thing," she said.

"Indeed," said Ariel, "for I can feel it from here. Can you tell me what it is?"

"Old Geni magic, Lady, for certain. Somewhere in those mountains the pigmen have found something better left alone. Give me a moment." She held her hands over the object and closed her eyes. A snarl of disgust crept over her face as she concentrated.

Trelanth thrust the amulet aside with a curse. "Forgive me, but I must cleanse myself. I will return shortly." With that she stood and left the room. No one spoke, they barely breathed, until she returned, wiping the water from her hands.

"Forgive me, my queen, I ..."

"Forgiven, dear friend. Tell me what you saw."

"There was a pigman, standing on a boulder, chanting something. Around his neck hung a sickly green stone that glowed weakly with power. Before him were hundreds of them, kneeling, bowing so their heads touched on the ground, worshiping him as a god, or master of some kind. Lady I was wrong at first, this thing isn't Geni magic, it's old demon magic."

"Demon magic," said Ariel as she gripped the mage by the arm. "How strong is it? Can you defeat it?"

"Oh yes, my queen, I can defeat it, for I have fought this kind of magic before. Get me face to face with this creature, and I'll make a swift end of him and his magic."

"Do you know where he is?"

"Somewhere in the mountains, but I couldn't pinpoint the location. "I'm certain, if I enhance one of Lady Freida's amulets, it will lead me right to him. The problem is his small army of followers. Lady, he had an Orc female captive that he was torturing. His stone draws power from the terror and life force of the victims."

"How well I remember," said Mearith, and Arlon nodded. "That's probably why they attacked Fugitive at that time of year. By the numbers Trelanth described, I'd say they're gearing up for another advance."

Ariel seemed lost in thought for a moment, then she banged her fist on the table. "I will not allow Fugitive to come under siege. This is my home, and we will defend it. It seems we have a task for Lord Tanis when he returns.

"Trelanth, prepare, for you will seek out this pigman mage and destroy him. Once that is accomplished, find the source of his power and make certain it cannot rise again for another to use. Lord Tanis will lead your warriors. The rest of us will prepare to defend Fugitive in case they slip around you and attack.

"Drakkat, prepare to bring all your people behind the walls ..."

"Forgive me, my queen, but the Scratite would prefer to remain outside the walls. The pigmen will avoid us, as our homes are surrounded by open fields. To engage us in battle would expose them before they're ready.

"No, if they come at all they will come from the trees. As soon as they attack the walls of Fugitive, the Scratite will strike them from behind. With us behind them, and the Lady Freida at the front, there won't be a lot for the rest of you to do."

Ariel chuckled and punched him lightly on the arm. "As you wish, my friend, but if Lady Freida thinks she's going to face them alone she is much mistaken, for I will be at her side."

"As will I," grinned Mearith. "However, we will prepare, but if I know Lord Tanis, the pigmen will never escape the mountains."

"That's the truth," said a soft voice. Mearith raised an eyebrow at the Elf who'd spoken. He grinned as he replied. "My Lord Tanis is a fierce warrior, and he is both fearless and tenacious. Unless you plan to ride with him, you'll be without much to do until he returns."

"You seem to admire and have a great deal of faith in him."

"I do, my queen. He will not fail you."

"When did he bring you out?"

"Two moon cycles past, my Lady. I've been training and hope to be allowed to join his band when he returns."

"That's little enough time for training, my friend," smiled Ariel, "but I will leave that decision up to Tanis. If he's willing to have you along, then I wish you well."

The room fell quiet then. Ariel sat listening to the soft voices all around her and smiled wistfully. Marc noticed her suddenly subdued mood and spoke. "My Lady, what troubles you?"

"I am home at last, Marc, and thrilled to be here, but I grieve, for the place is not the same without Randall."

"Lady, Randall is missed by all, for certain, but we do not yet know his fate. If you wish it, I'll set out for Shotar and see if I can determine if he yet lives."

"No, Marc, you are needed here. I ..." she got no further as the door banged open and Gormin entered with Randall, leaning on a cane.

"Randall," shouted Ariel, as she leaped to her feet and swept him into a hug. He grunted as she lifted him off his feet.

"Put him down, Ariel," called Mearith, "you're killing him."

Ariel set him back on his feet then leaned back to smile brightly at him. "It is so good to see you, dear friend. I was afraid we'd lost you."

"Queen Ariel, you're a sight for sore eyes. When that young pup came and burned us out I was afraid something had happened to you."

"Come, sit with us," she said, as she took his arm and led him to her table. Arlon rose and stepped away to make room for him. "Randall, had I known you had left Fugitive I would have cautioned Tanis to look for you."

"Perhaps it was better you didn't," he grinned as he carefully lowered himself to the bench. "As it is, I've learned much you should be aware of."

"Tell us, old friend," said Mearith as she passed him a pint.

He took a sip of the ale then began his tale. "Young Tanis hit us at dawn, raised bloody havoc, stole all the horses, ran off the cattle, and carried off the slaves. I'd tried to convince the fools to let the slaves go before something like that happened.

"He burned us out, so we all headed for Shotar. Once inside the walls we were questioned and then billeted in the slave pens. It seems there's not a lot of room to spare in the city of the king. The place is overflowing with armed men.

"The king cowers in his tower while every man able to bear arms is pressed into service, training for war. The gates have been thickened, and the walls braced. There wasn't a lot of food to go around, and, as more refugees came streaming in, we were pressed tighter and tighter together.

"Above that, it seems your efforts have impoverished many people while making still others rich. The sell price of a slave is now thrice what it was before you took Magdan. Tanis' efforts are adding to the value of a slave. This makes those who still own one even more determined to keep them.

"At the last of it, the women, children, and elders like me were shoved out through the gates to make room for the more able bodied who can bear arms to defend the city." Here he took another long pull from the tankard of ale.

"So, at that point I felt I'd learned all I could, what I needed to know. I gathered a few I felt I could trust, and we set out for Fugitive. There's about a dozen women and children outside being fed by Meg. Two more old geezers like me as well."

"Randall, it's so good to have you back with us," smiled Ariel. "It also appears that Lord Tanis has done his job well."

"Perhaps too well, my queen."

"Randall?"

"It was just a rumor, but a rumor can have some truth to it. It is said that a shipment of slaves will soon depart from Shotar to Magdan. It will appear to be over a hundred slaves with a hundred men at arms guarding them. In truth, there will be but twenty slaves and the rest will be men at arms in disguise."

"So, Tanis has done well, and now they seek to trap him," mused Mearith. "Randall, do you know when this will take place?"

"No, nor can I verify the truth of the rumor. I'd hoped to encounter him on the path here so I could warn him."

"He's due back here any day now. So, you left Fugitive to live in a village?" said Mearith. "My old friend, you don't fool me for a minute. You were scouting out the lay of the land for us."

Randall chuckled at that. "Yes, I was. Mearith, folks all too often discount the old and speak too freely in their presence. Marc has things under control here, so I thought I'd go do something useful."

"And you told no one what you were doing," said Ariel.

"Just Marc," grinned Randall. "The fewer who know a thing, the easier it is to keep it secret."

"Well, I, for one, am happy you've returned. Now you can help us prepare our defenses," smiled Ariel.

"Defenses, my queen? Do you believe Shotar will find us here?"

"You weren't here when the pigmen attacked?"

"No, Lady, I was unaware of a recent attack. I do see Telee has a shiny new sword though."

"My name is Freida now, Randall," she smiled. "Someone else must tell you how I came to possess both."

"As well as about the Lady Freida's new title," grinned Drakkat. He laughed as Freida punched his arm hard.

The evening wore on and Ariel basked in the love and companionship of her adopted home and friends. Tanis arrived with the dawn.

Into the Mountains

Tanis rode in with his near hundred new Bornani, as well as the original hundred fifty he'd started out with. The first thing he saw as he rode through the gate was Ariel and Mearith with Freida. He leaped from his horse and ran to them, dropping to one knee as he reached them. "Greetings, my queen. I believe we've been somewhat successful in the task you set for us."

"So I've heard," said Ariel, a twinkle in her eye. "However, it disturbs me to learn you've assumed the Title of Lord Commander without earning it properly."

He began to sputter an apology, but she held up her hand to stop his protest. Eline began to step forward, but Mearith waved her off, grinning. Ariel slowly held out her hand and Freida passed her the magic sword.

"Tanis of the Royal Guard," said Ariel, as she stepped closer to his kneeling form and placing the tip of the sword on his shoulder, "I Ariel, Queen of all Elfkind, do place upon you this magic sword and name you Lord Tanis, Commander of a Thousand." She touched his other shoulder with the sword then passed it back to Freida.

"Arise, Lord Tanis, Lord Arlon has a thousand Elves at Arms ready and awaiting you. Trelanth has a mighty task to complete, and I charge you to take your troops and defend her."

She helped him up then gave him a gentle hug. "You've done well, dear friend, and so you must again. Rest your people for this day, but be prepared to leave on the morrow. Trelanth will fill you in, and Arlon will introduce you to your aides." She winked at Mearith, then the three women walked away, leaving him standing there with his mouth hanging open.

Bewildered, Tanis stood watching the three women walk away. Arlon stepped up and grinned. "Come, my Lord Tanis, we have much to do."

"My Lord Arlon, what just happened?"

"In times past, one had to become leader of a thousand to gain the title of Lord Commander. After the war that broke the world, I was the only one of hundreds left alive to tell the tale.

"Our Lady Queen decided to stay with the traditional system, Tanis, and so, for this mission at least, you lead a thousand warriors of the combined forces. She has promoted you with full ceremony before royal witnesses as it was done in elder days.

"Come, I'll introduce you to your aides. There will be ten of them, eleven if you include Eline and her hundred plus. I assume you wish to take them with you."

Tanis mentally shook himself, struggling to get a handle on the situation. "Tell me, what was the old order of command? How did this work?"

"Traditionally, you would have an aide to lead each hundred of warriors. You would appoint a second to advise you and to relay commands to the aides. L'ark was my second, as you know. Maron has been acting as my second since L'ark was given a different mission by the queen. He now leads the hundred assigned to defend Fugitive."

"So, I'll have to choose a second?"

"Yes."

Tanis sighed and allowed his shoulders to slump. "I feel I'm in over my head here. Is there any helpful advice you can give me?"

"Stay confident, Tanis, speak with authority and confidence. Your people will respond to that. Show weakness, fear, or indecision, and you will lose them. They'll draw their confidence and strength from you."

Tanis looked thoughtful as he absorbed that. They passed through the gate and walked into the Elven encampment. There were close to two thousand Elves in all, counting the newly free slaves. At a signal from Arlon, the aides, six men and four women, rose and approached.

Arlon introduced Tanis as the newly raised Lord Tanis. They all knelt as one. "Hail Lord Tanis."

"Thank you, thank you all. Please rise. We seem to be missing someone. Bear with me a moment." He cupped his hands to his mouth and gave the cry of the hunting hawk.

Eline soon appeared and joined them, giving him the fist-to-shoulder salute. "Now we're all here."

"My Lord Tanis," said one of the aides, "this woman is only a leader of fifty."

"No longer," replied Tanis. "Eline, in my absence, you are now in command of the Reavers, a hundred fifty strong."

Again, she gave him the salute. "My Lord, I will strive to bring honor to the post."

"Now then, good people, fellow warriors. The queen has tasked me with leading you in the service of the Court Mage as she pursues a task of her own. I believe that, as soon as we return, I will be once again taking the Reavers out to harass the Geni, but for now, here we are."

"My Lord Tanis," said another, "who among us is to be your second?"

Tanis turned to Arlon. "You've led these folk for a long time, My Lord Arlon. Who would you recommend to be my second?"

Arlon showed no emotion at all as he spoke. "Since Eline leads the largest group in your army, she would be the natural choice, with Mexah as the next choice. However, these are your decisions to make."

"I will gladly trust your superior experience here," said Tanis. "Eline is my second with Mexah next in line. Now, until the Lady Trelanth comes to give us our marching orders, we might as well rest.

"Eline, I believe we'll be heading into the mountains. Tell Kern we'll be going on foot."

"You're not going to ride beside the Royal Mage?" asked another of the aides.

Tanis grinned at her. "You'll be running, the warriors will be running, and I'll run with you. I think I'm getting lazy, riding everywhere we go." There was a round of chuckles at that.

"All right, people, gather what weapons and supplies we need, then rest. I expect we'll be on the move soon enough."

He turned to walk away then, and grinned as he heard Eline behind him. "Mexah, you oversee the weapons, Gelia, you supervise the gathering of traveling rations. I'll bring the Reavers into the camp and make certain the healers have what they need before we set out."

Tanis grinned as he and Arlon headed back towards the inn. "Well, what do you think?"

"You did just fine, Tanis. I expected you'd want to keep your second in that position. Officially promoting her was a good touch."

"Will they work with her?"

"They will or I'll have their hides for it."

"No, I think she'll do just fine. Let her earn it, as I'll have to."

"Deciding to run with the troops instead of riding caught them by surprise," said Arlon. "They were expecting you to ride and themselves as well. I like this better. If you run as one of them then all the warriors will respect you. It was well done."

"Yes, well, I don't feel like a mighty lordling, nor do I want to have anyone else look at me as I once looked at the man who owned me. If all my warriors ride, I ride. If they run, then I run with them."

Arlon grinned and slapped him on the shoulder. "My Lady Queen has chosen well. It's good to have a brother-at-arms again. For far too long now I had no one to share concerns with, but carried the load alone."

Tanis gave him a strange look then sighed. "I think I got a taste of what you're saying as I led the Reavers. It all hangs from your shoulders, their success, their safety. Eline said it was good to have someone to talk to who you could trust. You had L'ark until the queen sent him to find her lost friend."

"That's true, Tanis. I have another second now, but that level of trust is still not the same because they still depend on you."

"And so the Lady Mearith always had her brother the king, Queen Ariel has Lady Mearith, but as the only surviving commander of a thousand you were somewhat isolated. I believe my sudden rise in status might have had something to do with that as well."

"Do you honestly think so?"

"Queen Ariel would be aware of this, Lord Arlon, and I'm quite certain she took it into account when she hatched the plot to increase my status."

"She increased your station, my friend, because you've earned it. You excelled as the captain of her guard, and as commander of the Queen's Reavers you've exceeded all expectation. Don't doubt her faith in you."

"Oh, I don't. I just hope it isn't misplaced."

"I'm quite sure it isn't, otherwise the Lady Mearith would sure have voiced an objection, but I was there when Queen Ariel got the idea, and Lady Mearith showed nothing but approval. Come on, I'll treat you to a pint and tell you of how a rescued slave became a smith out of legend and rose to be the adopted sister of the queen."

The gray light of early dawn saw a wave of armed Elves move away from the village of Fugitive and into the forest. They ran at an easy trot, headed for the mountains. Three days later they reached the high meadows and settled down for the night.

Trelanth, Ethor, Tanis, and his aides sat around one of the campfires. She was meditating and he was worrying. "Ethor, are you certain our campfires can't be seen?"

"They can't, my Lord Tanis. Trust me," he grinned.

"I am trusting you, with all our lives," he sighed.

"Relax, my Lord," said Eline. "Remember, it was Ethor who hid the passage of the Bornani from Magdan to Elfhome. All is well."

"Sorry, guess I'm a bit of a worrier."

"Yes, you are, but that's all right. Be at peace, my friends. I've ridden to battle with Lord Tanis before, and it's always the same. He worries, he fusses, then we make a plan, put it into action, succeed, and then move on to the next one."

"You seem pretty relaxed, Eline," observed one of the others.

"I am. You see our new Lord Commander as an untried leader, but that's not the case. He's earned his place, else the queen would have sent Lord Arlon or come herself.

"On our last mission, we formed and reformed several plans of attack, but, upon hearing of armed men waiting for us in the town, Lord Tanis made a new plan and into battle we went. We captured three towns at once and lost not a single warrior.

"Relax, my friends, let Lord Tanis do the worrying for us all."

"Shut up, Eline," grumbled Tanis. She chuckled and winked at the others, but said nothing.

Soon Trelanth opened her eyes, a snarl on her lips. "Lady?"

"All is well, Tanis, my friend, at least for us. Let me tell you this, torture is a useless tool, for it will rarely gain you accurate information. Torture for the purpose of gaining arcane power is far worse. It is abhorrent to me, for it brings the power of evil.

"This would-be mage we seek is drawing on that power. Somewhere he has managed to capture a number of people. I saw two Humans, an Elf, and five Orcs. He's slowly torturing to death each one in turn to draw their life force to him. He's also gathering more fighters into his army. They number in the many hundreds now."

"Can you lead us to him, Lady?"

"I can. The pathways are long and guarded. To pass through will mean fighting every step of the way. Worse yet, they'll know we're coming. Prepare yourselves, for tomorrow will see us encounter the first of the guarded pathways."

Tanis stared into the fire for a long moment before he spoke. "Forgive me, Lady Trelanth, but I'd far rather approach that mage and his hidden army from stealth. Can you describe the pathway we encounter on the morrow?"

"Describe it?"

"The road to it."

Perplexed, she gazed at him for a moment. "All right, we continue on the climb to the first pass. You saw that as we approached today. Once into the pass there is another small gap to the left. It climbs higher then drops down to a long narrow trail before opening up to a hidden valley cut by a small stream. At the other end of that valley is the second guarded pass."

Tanis turned to Eline. "Got all that?"

"Got it, my Lord."

"Send Dellan with fifty of the Reavers to clear that path. Tell him to wait for us in the hidden valley."

"On my way," she grinned, as she leaped to her feet.

"Ethor, go with Dellan, make sure the boar mage sees nothing."

"As you command, my Lord Tanis," he grinned, as he stood and hurried after Eline.

Trelanth was watching Tanis with an eyebrow quirked. "I thought it best if we could move along unhindered. Dellan will find the trail, eliminate the guards, and Ethor will make certain the event goes unobserved. Each time we approach a guarded area we will repeat this process."

"Excuse me, Lord Tanis."

"Mexah?"

"Forgive me, sir, but ..."

"You're afraid I'll let the Reavers have all the fun and all you'll get to do is carry supplies for them." The other Elf grinned sheepishly. "All right, Mexah, you know your warriors better than I do. Dellan is taking out the first group. You choose the next group, confer with Dellan to get a sense of what to expect, then send out your people.

"Eline will choose which of you savages will lead the group to follow Mexah, then the next." The wolfish grins that responded to that announcement made him chuckle.

"Lady Trelanth, we're surrounded by savage warriors, so it's quite safe for you to get some rest," said Tanis, as he rose to his feet.

"Where are you going?"

"Taking a turn at the watch."

"Lord Tanis," she smiled gently, "you have warriors to do that."

"Yes, and I want them well rested. I'll stand the watch in turn as will every other warrior under my command. There are no special favors here. You, my Lady, need to rest as this is your mission and ..."

"Yes, my Lord, I will rest." She grinned as she settled down beside the fire and closed her eyes.

A while later, fifty warriors silently passed his guard post and waved at him. Grinning, Tanis waved back. A moment later, Mexah arrived. "My turn," he said. "Get some rest, my Lord." Tanis gave him a friendly slap on the shoulder and returned to settle down for the rest of the night.

The sun was high overhead when they reached the entrance to the hidden pass the next day. They found a pile of dead bodies and a grinning Dellan waiting for them. "All clear to enter the high pass, my Lord," he grinned, as he gave Tanis the fist-to-shoulder salute.

Facing the Enemy

They crossed the long valley and passed through the next guarded point before stopping for the night. Another day, another guarded pass neutralized, and a full day of travel later brought them to the final pass. They settled down for the night while scouts slipped on ahead.

The next morning brought a surprise when the scouts returned. Ahead the land dipped down into a broad valley that held a large village of pigmen.

Tanis and Trelanth went to have a look for themselves. "It doesn't appear to be guarded," said Tanis, as they lay peering over a ridge and down into the valley below. "What do you want to do?"

"We have to get past them," she replied. "I'd prefer unseen if we can manage it. What think you?"

"I see two possibilities. One, we try to slip around them in the night."

"And the other?"

"We attack and eliminate them and, with them, much of the threat we face at Fugitive and as we pass through the mountains with newly freed Bornani."

"This village tells me they are becoming a full people, Tanis. Can we just completely destroy an entire people? Can you?"

"Lady Trelanth, you've said the boar mage is calling more warriors to him. This tells me that the village below isn't the only one. Destroying it would not eliminate an entire people."

"Look down there, Tanis, tell me what you see."

With a deep sigh, he began to tap his forehead on the ground. "Women and children," he replied softly as he lifted his head and met her eyes. "If not women and children, at least females and their young. I see no males and no warriors. This is your expedition, Lady Trelanth. What is your command?"

"Tanis, my friend, devise a way to pass this place without alarming our quarry, and preferably, without making war on women and children."

"They make war on us, use us for food."

"Is that reason enough to kill them all?"

Again he sighed. "No."

She was grinning at him now. "We need a third option."

"Then let's go back to camp and put all our heads together."

Back at the camp they called the aides together and filled them in. It was Ethor who had the solution. "My Lord, my Lady, give me fifty of the Bornani. We'll surround the village, keep anyone from leaving or sounding an alarm, but we won't harm anyone unless there is no other option. I can keep prying eyes from interfering."

Tanis looked to Trelanth who quirked an eyebrow at him. "All right, Ethor. Go to the Reavers and ask for volunteers. Surround them then we'll pass by."

The mage nodded then trotted away. Soon fifty warriors ran past and down into the valley, swiftly surrounding the village. Most of the pig people ran into their huts to hide, dragging the young ones in with them. Most but not all.

One large female grabbed a crude axe and ran screaming at the nearest Elf, Ethor. He simply pointed at the village and didn't move. She swung the axe, but he easily dodged and slapped her knuckles hard with the flat of his sword. She leaped away and stood glaring at him. He pointed back at the village.

With a snarl, she leaped at him again, swinging her axe with all her strength. He moved easily out of her path then slapped her hard on the rump with the sword. She spun and attacked again, but again she got her knuckles rapped, then spun about and a boot planted firmly on her butt.

She turned and glared at him, but he pointed to the village, tapped the point of his sword against her chest meaningfully, then pointed again. Watching him carefully, she backed away then returned to one of the huts.

To the man's surprise she soon returned, dragging a young one. She thrust the frightened child to him where it lay trembling at his feet. She bowed her head sadly and turned away. The child looked up to see him point at her retreating form. It took the hint.

As the child sped past her she spun around to gaze at him, bewildered. She pointed at the retreating child and grunted a single word. "Food."

"Not food," he replied.

"Why?"

"Not food. Child." She didn't seem to understand so he tried again.

"Child," he repeated, pointing to her belly.

Slowly the light of understanding reached her eyes. These warriors wouldn't kill her child. "Why?"

"Child," he replied.

She was mulling that over as the main army poured over the ridge and along the valley floor. She saw where they were going and spun back to him. She now understood what was going to happen. He saw as she accepted that and shifted her focus to her own survival and that of her village.

"No kill?" she asked, as she waved her hand to indicate the village.

"No kill," he replied.

"Why?"

"Not food, not enemy," he replied. He stepped closer and reached out to lightly tap her chest. "Not food." He then tapped his own chest. "Not food," he repeated.

Slowly the light of understanding reached her eyes. "Not food, not enemy." She turned and pointed into the mountain pass where the Elvish Army was disappearing from sight. Then she turned back. "Not food, enemy?"

"Yes, enemy."

"All kill?"

"All kill, enemy," he replied.

Again, he could see her mind struggling to grasp the situation. She now understood that all the males in the hidden valley would be killed, but there was still hope for the village, for the young and females. "No kill?" she asked as she once again swept out her hand to indicate the village.

"No fight, no kill," he replied.

She nodded slowly. "No food, no fight, no enemy?"

That made him smile. She understood at last. If her people didn't attack his for food, then there would be no killing. "No food, no fight, no enemy, no kill."

She nodded slowly then squared her shoulders. "Kekka," she said, as she thumped her chest.

His grin widened. "Kekka," he said, pointing at her. "Ethor." He pointed to his own chest.

"Etor," she growled. It was probably the best she would be able to do.

He nodded his delight and offered his hand. She eyed it suspiciously. He wiggled his fingers and raised his eyebrows at her. Slowly she extended her hand. He gripped it lightly for a moment. "Kekka, Ethor, friends."

She got the idea and grunted a word he didn't understand. He pointed back to her village. "Kekka go now, no kill, no enemy."

"Etor, no enemy, no food, no kill."

She nodded and turned away to where many of her people were watching them. She began to shout and they fearfully came out to her. Soon there was a lot of jabbering among them then Kekka returned. "No enemy, no kill. Kekka work?" She pointed to the small gardens near the huts.

"No kill, no enemy. Kekka work, stay close." She puzzled on that for a moment then nodded that she got the idea. Crouching, she quickly sketched a map of the village in the dirt. She indicated the small gardens. "Work." She swept her hand over the map. "Stay. Work," pointing to the gardens, "stay." She pointed to the village again. She had the idea.

Ethor nodded his approval and she trotted back to the others. Soon they all set to work tending the gardens. When darkness fell, they all retreated to their homes. The Elves slept in shifts, always plenty of guards awake and watching.

Shortly after dawn Kekka returned with a bowl of something steaming. She offered it to Ethor. "Food." He eyed it suspiciously. With a grunting chuckle, she pointed to the small gardens. "Food."

He could sense no poison nor any treachery from her, so he took his spoon from his belt and tasted the stew. Surprised at the taste, he gave her a nod of approval and ate the rest, returning the empty bowl to her.

She started away, but his voice brought her back. "Kekka?" She gave him a puzzled look. He patted his own chest. "Ethor, Elf." He then pointed to another Bornani, "Elf."

He repeated this process several times then waved his hand to indicate all his warriors. "Elf."

She worked on it for a moment then replied. "Etor, Elf." She waved her hand. "All Elf. All Etor folk Elf." His bright smile of approval told her she'd got it right.

"Kekka folk?"

"Coti," she replied. "All Kekka folk, Coti."

"Kekka, Coti fight Elf. Food. Why?"

She puzzled on that for a moment before answering. Finally, she spoke, certain that she understood the question. "Hungry. Need Food. Root gone. Hungry."

Ethor nodded thoughtfully as he absorbed that piece of information. These folk preferred roots and vegetation, but turned to meat to prevent starvation. Finally, he nodded that he understood.

She turned away and went back to her hut. Soon he saw her working at the garden. He wondered how Tanis and the others were faring.

WHILE ETHOR WAS TRYING to learn as much as possible about the Coti, Trelanth, Tanis, and his aides were peering over yet another ridge. They could see into a broad canyon below. There were hundreds of Coti camped there, all facing a cavern at the far end.

Just outside that cavern several captives were being held. As they watched, the Boar mage appeared from the cave and mounted the stone altar. He began to shout, and a green light flickered to life around him. An Elf captive was dragged to him, and he plunged a dagger into the victim.

Trelanth could see the flickering light slowly, reluctantly, moving toward him, feeding the green light that surrounded him. She started to rise, but Tanis caught her arm.

"Not just yet, Lady. Let me do this. I'll get you close enough to make an end of him and keep you safe at the same time." She gazed into his eyes for a long moment then nodded. They slipped back to the main army.

Tanis turned to Eline. "I make it nearly even in numbers. You?"

"Agreed, my Lord. It appears we are even in numbers. How do we approach this?"

Tanis quickly scraped together a mock-up of the canyon with his hands. "We're here," he said pointing out their position. All his aides watched carefully. "From the far side here, you could run down and attack, but not from the near side here. So, here's what we'll do.

"Eline, take three hundred and make your way around to the far side of the ridge. Mexah, you take another three hundred and man this side here.

"Eline, as soon as you're in position, have every man send a volley of arrows into their camp. Give them a ten count then send another volley.

"Mexah, as soon as Eline's second volley has them all facing her, you send them two volleys. As soon as the second one has flown bring your warriors back here.

"After Mexah's second volley of arrows has landed I'll lead the rest of the warriors through the gap and engage the enemy. Once they turn to face me, Eline, you lead your folk down the slope to join the battle.

"Mexah, when you arrive back here, your warriors bring the Lady Trelanth in to face the mage. Be sure to keep her safe, but don't get in her way either."

"Understood, my Lord."

"So, does everyone understand the battle plan?" There were nods of agreement all round. "All right then, let's go. Carefully now, they mustn't be aware of us until the first volley of arrows."

The aides swiftly spread the plan to their warriors, then, with no more sound than a sighing wind they rose and moved out. Tanis fussed quietly while they waited for the action to start, but there was no alarm raised. All eyes were on the mage and the screams of his victim.

Suddenly there was a great alarm as a rain of arrows fell from the sky. Dozens of Coti fighters fell to that rain. Before they could see the direction of the danger another rain of death fell. They all turned to face that canyon wall and take cover.

As the Coti took cover, Mexah's troops stood and sent a volley of arrows down on the hapless Coti. Terrified and confused they turned to face yet another rain of death. By this point their numbers had been cut in half, and then Tanis screamed his challenge.

Hundreds of Elvish warriors poured through the gap and into the canyon, killing as they went, Tanis leading the charge. Confusion and terror reigned as the Coti leaders struggled to gain some control and face this new enemy. That was short lived as Eline and her warriors poured down the steep slope and joined the fray.

Understanding finally broke through the mage's concentration and he released his victim, dropping him to the ground as he began a spell cast. A sickly green bolt of light left his hands and an Elf warrior exploded in green dust mixed with blood.

The mage prepared another bolt, but it fizzled in his hands. Horrified he looked up to see an Elf mage striding towards him. She waded through the mad melee with hundreds of Elvish warriors cutting a path for her and protecting her passage. He turned and fled into the cavern.

As she reached the bloodied altar, Trelanth spoke to the Elf beside her. He began to shout orders and his troops swiftly surrounded the captives and defended them, driving back any attempts to reach the cavern. Trelanth entered alone.

Inside the cavern, she could hear him chanting. The huge room was lit with a sickly green light. With a single spoken word, she filled the space with bright clear light, bringing a shriek of fear from the mage. A huge green boulder glowed with power and fed it to the mad creature. He sent a bolt of light at her.

Trelanth staggered back from the power of that blow, but she raised her shield in time. With a snarl, she brushed aside the next attempt. Thrusting out her hand, Trelanth spoke a single word and the mage began to crumple in on himself, shrieking and screaming as a force too strong to be believed slowly crushed the life out of him.

She held the force on him until there was nothing left but a small stain on the cavern floor. At that point the green stone began to move, change, and rise from the ground. "As I thought," said Trelanth. "Come, old Demon, meet your fate as did all your kin so long ago."

The misshapen creature leaped at her with terrifying speed, but it was stopped cold by her shield. She closed her eyes and began to chant. "Nooooo," came the rasping denial from the mouth of the beast.

Trelanth ignored it and began inscribing runes on the ground, her sweet voice continuing her chant. The demon went wild as it attacked with the mad fury of whatever hell had spawned it so long ago. It was all in vain.

Her chant continued as the circle of runes on the ground grew until it was a full circle. She stopped chanting and opened her eyes. "Will you return of your own free will, or will I send you myself?"

"Perhaps there's another way, great mage," oozed a sickly voice as the demon ceased its useless assault on her shield. "Imagine, if you will, the power you could access with my strength added to yours. You could ..."

Trelanth spoke a single word and the demon screamed in protest as the ground opened up and swallowed it whole. She stepped out of her circle of runes, and it moved of its own accord, shifting to fully cover the place where the demon had disappeared.

"What in the name of all creation was that thing?"

She turned to see Tanis standing behind her, a bloody sword in his hand. "It was a demon. Somehow it managed to avoid the fate suffered by its brethren when Queen Onlay broke the world. It probably slept here until that pigman found it. It twisted and corrupted his mind, but no more.

"Outside now, quickly. I'll bring down the mountain on this place so no other will ever discover what happened here."

"I must say, Lady Trelanth, that was impressive," said Tanis, as they left the cavern together.

"I've fought them before, Lord Tanis. This one wasn't nearly as powerful as he thought he was. So, I see you have things well under control out here."

"It's done, finished, Lady. The pigmen are defeated, most are dead, with only a few escaped into the mountains."

"How did our people fare?"

"We have thirteen dead and another sixty-some wounds."

"My Lord Tanis, you're a complete marvel. You've defeated an entire army with so few casualties. Bring the dead to me here; I will release their spirits back into the great forest where they can rest before returning to us one day."

It was quickly done, and as Trelanth performed the ceremony all could see the bodies slowly turn to a golden mist then rise into the air and vanish into the sky, slowly moving in the direction of the forest they'd left behind just a few days before. When it was done, they gathered their wounded and set out for Fugitive.

Early the next morning there was a wave of Elvish warriors moving past the village. As they ran, Tanis noticed Ethor in conversation with one of the females.

"Etor folk go?"

"We go. No harm Kekka folk. Friends now."

"Friends now."

Together they watched the Elves move swiftly through the valley and back into the mountain pass. Ethor's guards were the last to leave and then he passed her a thick bladed steel knife before he joined them. "Strong. Cut roots. Food faster." She gazed in wonder as he trotted away after his people.

That night, as they camped and had fires for the first time in many days, Tanis called him over. "My Lord?"

"Ethor, did I see you having a conversation with one of the pigman females?"

"Coti, my Lord. Their people call themselves Coti. Yes, Kekka is the village leader. She's smarter than we believed. Language is difficult for them as their jaws don't quite work right for it, but they're intelligent."

Trelanth was grinning at him and he blushed. "So share with us, Ethor, what did the woman tell you, or is that a private matter?"

"Trelanth, so help me, Royal Mage or not, ..." he shook a threatening finger at her.

She burst out laughing. "Peace, old friend, peace. Tell us what you learned."

He shook a finger at her again then grinned sheepishly. "She's clever and she caught on quickly. First, she tried to fight me. I imagine that was her duty as village leader. When I wouldn't kill her, she brought me a young one to kill and eat. She believed that was why we were there.

"When I refused to eat the child, but let him go, she wanted to know why. We went from there. I learned they prefer to eat roots they find in the forest or grow themselves."

"Did you find out why they attack us for food?"

"When food supplies run low they hunt for meat, any meat. Once the Mage arose they began to hunt for Elves, Humans, Dwarves, Orcs, any and all they encountered. They're angry, and vengeful. They know they were created from a food animal, and they resent those who once fed on their kind.

"I believe I managed a truce with this village anyway. We agreed that neither of us is food, nor are we enemies. Kekka can't speak for any other besides her village, but we have nothing to fear from them at least."

"Seriously? You believe there can be peace with the pigmen?" asked Tanis.

"Coti, my Lord, and yes, I believe we can find enough common ground to make peace with them. She was able to understand the concept of slave, equating it to a food source. Through that she found a kinship with us.

"I have no idea at all if the rest of her kind will understand. However, with what happened to the mage and his army, it shouldn't be hard for Kekka to convince the rest of them that a peace with the Elves is a safer road to walk."

Tanis sighed and gazed into the fire without speaking. "Tanis?"

"Yes, Trelanth?"

"What's going through that mind of yours?"

"I was just musing over how close I came to ordering the total destruction of that village. That act would have deepened the resentment against us, and reinforced the notion that Elves are deadly enemies to be killed.

"You stopped me and demanded another option, a better way to attain our goals. As a result of that, Ethor has gained much useful information and sown the seeds of a peace between us and the Coti.

"People, I learned well the lessons of resentment and hatred as a slave. Queen Ariel set me free, and I found I have a knack for tactics of war. However, Lady Mearith once told me to learn as much as I could about everything. She said the more a person knows the better.

"Trelanth, you gave me a lesson in compassion, and Ethor has shown me the possibilities of that. I think perhaps there's more here I can learn, and in so doing, the better I can serve the queen and all Elves."

Trelanth reached over to give his shoulder a gentle squeeze. "Tanis, my friend, a man who can admit he still has much to learn is already a wise man. We've all learned much from you on this quest as well.

"Had we fought our way through, as I expected we'd have to do, we'd have arrived with fewer warriors than we did, and those who did arrive would have been weary from battles already fought. Even then, we'd have faced an enemy who was aware of us and holding the superior position. That village would have been destroyed as well."

Tanis smiled shyly and nodded. "Ethor, did I see you give her something as you parted?"

"Yes, my Lord. I gave her a heavy knife. It's not a dagger, nor would it be of much use as a weapon, but it will make her life a lot easier when chopping root vegetables. As a mage, I used it for chopping herbs and roots in preparing potions."

"And as a token of friendship you used it to increase the understanding between our peoples. Ethor, my friend, remind me to pay closer attention to your counsel in future."

"Get some rest, my Lord," smiled Ethor.

Tanis sighed deeply then settled back. "Perhaps I'll do just that. Somebody wake me for a turn at watch."

Several days later they arrived back at Fugitive to find the people there engaged in a pitched battle.

Under Siege

L ife at Fugitive had been quite peaceful, and Ariel was getting anxious for Tanis to return. She was growing uneasy as was Mearith. As they stood atop the wall early one morning Ariel spoke of it. "What is it, my heart? You seem restless?"

"I am, my delight. I'm getting that old itch again. Something is amiss somewhere."

"I agree, but I checked on Trelanth last night. I saw them returning victorious, yet my friends and protectors still stay more alert than usual." Ariel gently gripped the stone that hung about her neck.

"Oh?"

"Yes. It keeps showing me a strange creature, but I don't know why."

Mearith was suddenly fully alert. "Can you describe it?"

"It's long and sturdy of body," replied Ariel, "yet covered with scales. Its movements are sinuous and it keeps its face close to the ground as though tracking prey. Mearith, its face is almost like the face of an Elf."

Mearith began to swear as she leaped down the steps from the wall, bawling for Arlon. He appeared from the inn and ran toward them. "Arlon, the queen's had a vision of a hunting Telf. Get scouts out a lot farther than they are. Somebody fetch Drakkat."

She was still muttering as Arlon sped away and Ariel caught up to her. "Mearith, what is a Telf?"

"Forgive me, Ariel. What you saw was indeed a Telf, a creature created from several others plus a minor demon. The Geni made them to terrorize the Elves, thus the name. That thing will track an Elf across the most unforgiving terrain. It will never stop, and it will never rest until it has found and killed its quarry.

"I'd say the Geni have either made one, or they managed to keep some of them alive. I'd wager one of the Geni has given it the scent of a slave Tanis brought out, otherwise you'd have seen it sooner. If that's indeed what's happening that accursed thing will lead them right to Fugitive.

"My love, can you call the image without the Geni seeing you?"

"Yes." Ariel pulled out the jewel from around her neck and held it in her hand. "Now, my old friend, show me this abomination. Show me where it is and what it's about."

Slowly the vision came to her. The creature was tracking through the forest, its face close to the ground, and an armored Geni holding a strong leash being pulled along. Ariel pulled back and widened the vision. She gasped as she saw the armed men and Orcs marching along behind.

A snarl crossed her face as she released the vision. By now all her advisers had gathered in the square with her, quietly awaiting her orders. "They're coming," she said, as she returned the stone to her tunic.

"Ariel, what did you see?" asked Mearith.

She raised her head and spoke to the gathered people. "A Geni leads men-at-arms, hundreds of them, through the forest. Something called a Telf is tracking us, bringing them here. They will arrive before nightfall. Mearith, take command and prepare our defenses."

Mearith was in action instantly. "Arlon, are those scouts out there?"

"They are on the way, Lady."

"Drakkat, bring your people inside the walls. We'll help you rebuild when the battle is over. Gormin, are your dams ready?"

"Aye, they are, but not helpful unless they come through the swamp."

"How strong are the walls?"

"These are Dwarven built walls, Mearith, timber and stone," grinned Gormin. "They'll hold, and they won't burn."

"Marc, are the people ready?"

"We are." Turning he began to shout orders. "Man the walls, prepare to brace the gate. Get all the arrows, stones, and oil to their stations. Orcs with axes prepare to repel ladders."

"Arlon, they have a Telf with them, be wary. You know what to do."

"Yes, Lady Mearith, I know. We've fought these things before, you and I. I'll take the Elves into the forest now. How many will you want here to protect the queen?"

"Protect the queen?" asked Ariel, raising an eyebrow at him.

"Forgive me, Lady Ariel, but I assumed you would not abandon Fugitive and retreat into the mountains until the battle is over."

"Your assessment is correct," she grinned. "I will remain here to defend my home."

"Take your warriors into the trees, Arlon," said Drakkat. "They'll be more effective from there. The Scratite will be the queen's guard." Arlon nodded and trotted away.

As Arlon left Rolfin, the Dwarven smith, shyly approached. "Lady Ariel."

"What is it, Master Smith?"

"It's Freida, Lady ..."

"Take me to her." He led her to the forge where Freida was cowering behind a pile of iron ore.

"Freida?"

"They're coming, aren't they," she sniffed, trembling. "The masters, they're coming. I knew they would. They always do, they find us and ..." her voice trailed off.

Ariel reached for her hands and pulled her to her feet. "Hush now, my beloved sister, hush now. Yes, they're coming, but they'll get a shock when they arrive. We are no meek slaves to be dragged back and beaten.

"I am Ariel, Queen of the High Born returned. You are my sister, Freida of the god sword, the sword that can never know defeat. Come, Freida, with Mearith at my right hand and you at my left we will drive them back behind the walls of Shotar. We are no longer escaped slaves, we are the Bornani. Come."

Reluctantly, Freida allowed herself to be taken out into the sunshine. Ariel watched as, slowly, the crippling fear left Freida's eyes to be replaced with a terrible burning rage. "Yes, come to me, masters of slaves," she muttered. "Come meet the god sword. I have trembled in fear of you for the last time."

The day wore on in preparations for the oncoming battle. Ariel cursed herself for sending most of her best warriors with Trelanth, leaving Fugitive somewhat vulnerable. She knew it was wrong, but she vowed to use all the power given her by the ancient queen to defend the place she now called home. She would only use that power as a last resort, but she would use it.

The day was well along when a single Borni raced from the forest and across the fields, past the empty houses of the Orcs, and straight through the gates of Fugitive. Dropping to one knee he spoke to the queen. "Lady Ariel, the enemy is right behind me. There were close to a thousand men at arms."

"But no longer?"

"They're a hundred fewer now, my queen," he grinned. "These are hardened and disciplined warriors, Lady. As the volley of arrows felled them they dismounted and set up a shield wall. They didn't try to pursue us into the forest. The Geni mage created a shield then they set out again."

"Rise, my friend. Catch your breath then rejoin Arlon in the forest. I'll deal with this Geni."

As the man trotted away Ariel called for the gates to be closed then climbed back to the wall where Freida was still pacing. Mearith was right at her side. They stood watching, knowing the direction from which the enemy would come.

"Ariel, my delight?"

"I know, dear heart. I will deal with the Geni, but no more unless needed. The Elves must find their own strength. Stay by my side now, keep me grounded."

The attacking force spilled from the forest, led by the Geni still holding the leash of the beast. He waved his hand and several men rode out to set the huts of the Scratite Orcs ablaze. "Huh, saw that coming," grunted Drakkat, as he watched helplessly.

Saggit was beside him. "I brought the hearth stone inside with me. We will rebuild, my brother."

"The Elves will help you," said Ariel.

"And now comes the disgusting part," growled Mearith.

"Mearith?"

"Yes, now the mighty Geni will approach, but well out of bow shot, and tell us, at great length, how it will be in our best interest to send out all the freed slaves. All the Humans and Orcs will be rewarded and all crimes forgiven. Blah, blah, blah."

"Perhaps we can shake his confidence a bit," grinned Ariel. She slipped her bow from her shoulder and nocked an arrow.

The Geni stopped well away from the wall, holding back the struggling beast. The Telf fought the restraining leash, screaming like a child being tortured. The Geni silenced it with a word then called out to the people on the wall.

"Hear me, people of Fugitive, you have been found, as you knew you would be. Your Elf Queen is in the mountains, dealing with an apprentice of mine. She cannot help you. Send out the stolen slaves and no harm ..."

He got no further as an arrow streaked from the wall. He threw up his magic shield, but the arrow wasn't meant for him. The beast in front of him suddenly reared up, gurgling and fighting to pull out the arrow from its throat. As it sank to the ground, dead, the Geni hastily backed his horse further from the wall.

Ariel grinned as she drew another arrow. "You'll need to get further away than that to escape me, Geni," she said, nocking the arrow.

The Geni continued to back away, but a huge Orc rode forward. "Magic and arrows are the weapons of cowards and children," he roared. "Is there none within those walls who will fight with honor?"

Drakkat stepped to the top of the wall. "Those who ride with Geni have no honor," he shouted back.

The big Orc dismounted and stepped forward. "I am Kettar, Chieftain of Tomak Clan. By my word of honor, the Geni will not interfere. Name yourself and your clan."

"I am Drakkat, Chieftain of Scratite Clan. I serve the Elf Queen, but I give you my word, she will not interfere."

"Then come out, face me as a warrior, not an Elf fighting from hiding."

"I come," replied Drakkat. "You have until I reach the gate to flee behind the Geni."

"Drakkat ..."

"It is a challenge of honor, my queen. I can't refuse, and I beg you not to interfere."

"Just be careful, come back to me in one piece."

He gave a wolfish grin then trotted down the steps to the ground and headed for the gate. "I'm surprised he didn't jump off the wall," said Freida.

"His opponent is bigger and stronger," grinned Saggit. "He's overconfident and Drakkat will play on that. Watch now, my queen, and see the true power of your friend, our Chieftain."

"You won't mind if I make sure the others don't interfere," replied Ariel.

"They won't, Lady, for if they try the Orcs will turn on them and they know it."

Ariel watched with baited breath as Drakkat stepped through the gate and faced the bigger Orc. "For the honor of the clan," shouted Kettar.

"For the honor of the clan," replied Drakkat.

The two combatants ran at each other. The bigger Orc swinging both swords in a curtain of steel and Drakkat wielding his huge axe. They collided and Drakkat was sent sprawling, but one of other man's swords was broken. He cast it aside and waited for Drakkat to get up.

They nodded to each other and charged. Again, Drakkat was sent flying to land heavily, bleeding slightly from a small cut on his shoulder. He rolled to his feet, shook it off, and came in again.

Ariel was terrified for her friend as his bigger opponent continued to batter him down. Time and time again the huge Orc knocked him down, but he kept getting back up. "He's getting killed," said Ariel. "Can't we do something?"

Beside her Saggit just chuckled. "Get on with it, brother, the show has gone on long enough," he growled. "Our Lady Queen is getting fretful. If you play with him any longer she might lose control."

"What do you mean, play with him," demanded Ariel, as she grabbed Saggit by the shoulder.

"Watch now, Lady Ariel. Just as Kettar always lets him up when Drakkat falls, Drakkat allows him the better of the exchange. The Orc doesn't live who could best Drakkat in battle."

Ariel turned back to the fight to see Drakkat and the big Orc charge again. This time Drakkat ducked beneath the sword stroke and smashed the flat of his axe into his opponent's face. He then spun about and the axe separated the head from the shoulders of his opponent.

Drakkat stooped, swept up the huge sword, and then stood over the fallen warrior, his arms raised high in victory. "He fought with honor," he shouted. "This day I have slain a great chieftain. Those who rode with him can speak of him with pride."

Forty of the Orcs dismounted and approached Drakkat. "You fought with honor, great chieftain," said one. "You've claimed the Sword of Tomak. It has never, before this day, left the clan that created it. It's a great prize, treat it with respect and know, one day, another will come to reclaim it."

"He was a great chieftain and a mighty warrior," replied Drakkat. "I hold the axe of the Scratite, and I know its worth. I keep no trophies. The sword should remain with its people." He passed it, hilt first, to the man who'd spoken.

Dumbfounded, the Orc accepted the sword from Drakkat. "You return the sword to the clan?"

"Your chieftain fought with honor; the sword should remain with you. Having said that, I'm always willing to accommodate a challenge of honor."

The man grinned then looked to his comrades. They nodded and he turned back to Drakkat. "Our clan is small, but we live by the old codes. Would you consider absorbing us into your clan?"

"I serve the Elf Queen, not the Geni."

The other snorted in disgust. "The Tomac have no love of the Geni."

"This valley is broad enough for a few more," grinned Drakkat. "I accept you. Go from this place, gather your families and return. We will rebuild and you can help us."

"Do you not trust us to fight at your side?"

Drakkat looked them over for a moment then nodded. "Inside then, you will defend the gate." They grinned as they returned to their horses, then suddenly raced towards the walls of Fugitive. Drakkat ran ahead of them. "Allies, open the gate. Allies, open the gate."

"Do it," shouted Marc.

"Marc?"

"Do it, get that gate open for them." The gates swung open for the fleeing Orcs who had the entire army in pursuit. Once inside they leaped from their horses and helped brace the gates.

The onrushing army reached the wall to face a hail of arrows, heavy stones, and horse droppings thrown from above. When they realized the Geni mage hadn't created a shield to protect them, they withdrew out of bow shot. There they found their Geni mage, dead with an arrow through the heart.

Ariel and her advisers had returned to the inn as soon as the enemy retreated, and darkness fell. Ariel looked up as Drakkat entered with another Orc in tow. They both knelt before her. "Rise, my friends. Drakkat, who have you brought to me?"

"Lady, this day I accepted the challenge of the Tomac chieftain and defeated him. I then absorbed the Tomac into Scratite Clan. This is Horak, who now speaks for the Tomac."

"I greet you, Horak. Drakkat has brought you to me, and he appears to trust you, and so, I will also if you swear on your honor and that of your clan to be loyal to me."

"That is why I have come, Elf Queen, to swear my loyalty and that of my clan. I swear on my honor and that of my clan to serve you as you command."

"I accept you, Horak, and your clan. Tell me, what of the army which faces me?"

"There are about a hundred-fifty career soldiers, Lady, the rest are conscripts, poorly trained, but well-armed and vengeful."

"Vengeful?"

"Aye, Lady," he grinned. "Many were wealthy, and sons of the wealthy, but it seems your activities have impoverished them somewhat. You know, slave owners, slave breeders, and the like. Wealthy farmers. There are also about a hundred-fifty more Orcs, mercenaries and brigands, for the most part."

"Could we sway them to our side, do you think?"

"Easily, if you pay them enough, Lady, but you'd never be able to trust them."

"Understood. So be it then. Darkkat is now your chieftain?"

"He is that."

"Then I leave you in his hands. Do you have family? A mate left back in the city? I assume this force has come from Shotar."

"Yes, we rode out from Shotar as soon as the mage managed to get control of the abomination. Killing that was a boon to the world. Yes, Lady, I have a mate and child back in Shotar. Several of the others also."

"Tell me why you rode out with this army."

"Food and other resources are scarce in the city, Great Queen. Those who take up arms in the service of the king get preference over those who cannot."

Ariel nodded as she absorbed this information. "Drakkat, remind me, once this is over, to devise a way to get these folks' families out of that accursed city."

He grinned and nodded. "With pleasure, my queen. Lady, I assume that army is not destined to return."

"No, they found their way here, but, like the battle of the snows, they will not return."

"Be wary of the Geni, Lady Queen," said Horak. "That one is a powerful mage."

"He is already dead," she replied. "Just as my first arrow pierced the beast and took its life, so my second took the life of the mage. My bow is also magic, a special gift from the greatest of the Borni warriors. My arrow will travel to its target no matter how far away or how well shielded.

"When they find his body, will they now try to return to Shotar?"

"No, Lady. The command now falls to a human soldier named Maxwell. He lost his entire fortune when you took the city of Magdan. He will pursue you unto death."

"Then I will grant him his wish. Thank you, Horak, and welcome to the clan. Drakkat, see to your new people, then return to me for a council of war."

"You know what to do," said Drakkat, as he gave the other Orc a friendly clap on the shoulder. Horak grunted an acknowledgment and left.

Ariel then turned to Mearith. "What's our next move?"

"They'll come at us at first light. They're in the trees now, cutting rams to batter down the gate."

"Cutting trees?"

"Yes, but Arlon will see that they pay dearly for that offense. In the morning, they will attack on foot, for horses are useless against a wall. Men will carry the rams and others will hold shields over their heads to protect them from stones and arrows.

"While those men attack the gate, others will bring up ladders to scale the walls. That's when Arlon will strike them from behind. They'll be jammed between the walls and the Elves.

"There they will perish," said Ariel. "They will not scale the wall for you and I along with Freida, Gormin, Drakkat, and the good men of Fugitive will be there to prevent that from happening. Get some rest, my people. Korath, take the guard and man the walls. Let us know if anything goes amiss." He nodded as he rose and left the inn.

All through the night the Elves atop the wall watched the campfires of the enemy. They'd heard the ring of the axes in the forest and the screams of the dying as the Borni defended the trees.

Dawn came cold and misty. Out of that gray mist charged the enemy army, carrying the one lone ram they'd managed to cut. It had cost them dearly. "Brace the gate, man the walls," came the call from the watch post.

By the time the ram first touched the gate several men had fallen to arrows and stone, the gates were well braced and the walls fully manned. The ram bounced back from the gate, but the plan went to hell from there. Freida, stripped to the waist, leaped from the wall and into the mass of soldiers below.

Singing at the top of her lungs, Freida slew those closest to her. She was unaware of Ariel and Mearith beside her. Drakkat and the royal guard joined them, and mayhem ensued.

Startled by the ferocity of the Elf woman's attack, several men-at-arms fell to the god sword. No shield nor armor could stand before that sword as the blade sliced through all before it. It was the sheer numbers of opponents facing them that eventually stopped them and forced them back towards the wall.

It was looking bad when the gates suddenly swung open and the Tomac Orcs came boiling out. They fought their way towards the queen and her party just as Arlon and the Elves struck from behind. Madness ensued, and in that madness the Tomac reached Ariel and surrounded her.

Together they retreated to the gates, Ariel dragging Freida all the way. She was still spoiling for a fight as they got her back inside and the gates closed behind her. Freida saw Mearith grinning at her. "What?"

"Remind me to teach you some battle tactics, my sister." Freida sighed and let her shoulders droop as she blushed. Mearith hugged her then patted her shoulder. "Come on, Ariel is already atop the wall once again."

Mearith raced up the steps to find Ariel, bow in hand, still carrying the fight to the enemy. Arlon's Elves had struck and then fled back toward the forest. That's when the army realized the Elves had already stolen all the horses. Some broke and tried to pursue.

That's when Freida leaped off the wall again, Ariel, Mearith, and Drakkat right beside her. Once again, the god sword sang its song of death and men-at-arms fell back before the sheer madness and ferocity of her attack. The Elves returned, the gates opened again with men and Orcs pouring out. That's when Tanis and his thousand warriors arrived.

The battle was soon over, the dead and dying piled high on the field before the walls of Fugitive. "Some escaped to the forest," shouted Ariel. "Arlon, run them down, find them, slay them, none can escape."

Arlon and hundreds of Elves swept from the battle ground to hunt down those who fled the field. The location of Fugitive had to remain secret. Tanis and Trelanth went to report to Ariel while Marc directed the looting of the bodies then the cleaning up of the area.

Once the bodies had given up their booty, they were hauled away and dumped into the great swamp. When it was done, the Dwarves broke the dam, and the bodies were washed away. Even if any were to be found, there would be no way to determine from whence they came.

A New Battle Plan

Ariel and her closest advisers were gathered at the inn where Tanis and Trelanth gave their report. When they finished, Ariel smiled. "Well done, dear friends, well done indeed. It appears that the Geni were fostering the pigmen as random warriors." She turned to Ethor. "So, you managed to speak to them? They have language? They're actually a people?"

"Yes, my queen. They're called the Coti. Their language is rudimentary, a version of the Common Tongue, but they can reason and understand if given time. They build homes and raise crops, preferring to eat roots rather than meat.

"They only hunt when the crops run out late in winter. Once the mage came to them he convinced them to attack anything that moved, reminded them they were once a food source for all."

"And you believe you've changed that?"

"No, Lady, but I have sown the seeds of doubt and made a friend. We didn't destroy the village, refused to kill any of the young for food, and left them in peace as we departed their high valley.

"Lady, I believe, that with a bit of effort, I can work out an alliance with that village."

"An alliance?"

"Perhaps a truce would be a better word."

Ariel smiled at the earnest Elf. "Tell me what you have in mind, Ethor."

"Lady, the Reavers raid the farms far and wide. We take the horses, run off the livestock, and burn the homes. As the season wears on there should be plenty of root crops left unattended. If we loaded a few pack horses and delivered them to the Coti village they might pass the winter in relative ease.

"The idea, my queen, is to enlist their help in securing safe passage through the high passes to the first waystation. One of the warriors told me how to find it. If we could provision these Coti and enlist their help as mountain guides and scouts ..."

"I see what you have in mind, Ethor. Tanis, what think you?"

"I like the idea, my queen. I'd far rather have these Coti watching out for us than hunting us. With no battles to fight and no enemies to watch for, the first leg of the journey to Elfhome would be made more swiftly."

"Mearith?"

"So, they've become a people," she mused. "Ethor has the right of it. If they are now a true people in their own right, then we must do all we can to make them our allies, not tools of the Geni.

"However, one thing bothers me. The wild boars from which they were created are creatures of the forest, not the mountains. How is it they ended up there, trying to scratch a few roots from poor thin soil in shorter summers."

"I asked Kekka that," replied Ethor. "She said they'd had nowhere else to go. After the war that broke the world they did retreat to the forests, but were hunted for food by those Orcs and Men who were left alive and trying not to starve. They were driven to the mountains where they managed to survive.

"She said the Geni made them, but they hate the Geni for only partly giving them form. It seems the boars were already fairly intelligent, all the Geni did was give them humanoid form and weapons. The rest they've done themselves over time."

Ariel turned to Arlon. "What say you?"

"I agree with Tanis, Lady. Better an ally than an enemy through those narrow mountain passes."

"Randall, Marc?"

"They're right, Ariel," grinned Randall. "Besides, then we wouldn't have to worry about an attack from that quarter." Marc nodded his agreement.

"Gormin? I can hear your mind working from here."

He chuckled at that. "Aye, Lady. Ethor, you say they only use stone tools; they have no knowledge of iron."

"None that I could see. I gave Kekka a thick knife for chopping vegetables and she was amazed at it."

"Hmm," grunted the old Dwarf. "I'm just wondering if we might be able to make miners and smiths out of them. Failing that, perhaps we could find a place to rebuild our own lost city, supplying the Coti with metals in exchange for them growing food for us."

"Forgive me, friend Dwarf," grinned Mearith, "but aren't you the one who challenged them by shouting you loved the taste of pork?"

"Aye, well," chuckled the old fellow, "I thought it better to enjoy some roast pork than to be enjoyed as roast Dwarf."

"Can't argue that," chuckled Marc. "But now we have another problem."

"The boy's right," said Randall. "I'm quite certain the Geni now know the path to Fugitive. For all we know there could be another force on their way as we speak."

"Then we must change that path," said Trelanth, as she rose to her feet. "With your permission, Lady, I and my mages will be about the task."

"Will the four of you be enough?" asked Ariel.

"Aye, Lady, more than enough."

"You'll need protection," said Ariel. "How many do you need?"

"The Reavers should be more than enough, my queen."

"Tanis, send them, but I want you to remain here to advise me. We must devise a new battle plan in light of new information we've gathered."

Tanis nodded then rose and stepped to the door. "Eline," he called. She was there instantly. "Lady Trelanth has another errand. Take the Reavers and see she stays out of trouble."

"With great pleasure, Lord Tanis. Are we running or riding this time?"

"Kern's getting fat with nothing to do, take the horses."

With a laugh, she was gone and he turned back to resume his place at the long table.

"All right, good people," said Ariel, as soon as Tanis had resumed his seat, "now we get to it. The original plan was to fill the cities with refugees, placing a heavy drain on their resources. From what Randall has discovered, we know Tanis has been extremely successful at that. However, this is creating another problem I had not foreseen.

"The Geni are pressing every Human, Orc, and Dwarf able to bear arms into service, feeding them and starving those who cannot fight. If the other cities are following the same policy, and I'm sure they will be, it will be a lot harder to capture one and free the slaves.

"So, we need a new plan. I'm wide open to suggestions, my friends. We need to free those slaves, but I'd rather do it with as little loss of life as possible. Help me here, what do you think we should do next?"

They all looked thoughtful, and Tanis turned to Randall. "Tell me how it is in the city, Randall, for the slaves, I mean."

"Well, perhaps a bit better than before, in truth." Ariel raised an eyebrow at him. "You see, Lady, because of what you've done, there is a shortage of able-bodied slaves. They've become extremely valuable, and, since all they eat is oshar, they're no drain on the food resources."

"What's going through that head of yours, Tanis my friend," asked Mearith.

"Well, Lady, it seems the Reavers were successful. Now the city is full and struggling. As the season wears on it will only get worse. Once the winter comes that will magnify even more. By the time next spring arrives, the men-at-arms within the walls will be weakened from hunger and more. Eventually the city will have to send them out to gather food, if nothing else.

"They'll be vulnerable then. That's when we take them down. Lady, it might take a year or two, but eventually we could empty a city of fighters, leaving it open for the pickings.

"I suggest we split our warriors into several raiding groups like the Reavers. Instead of just filling Shotar with refugees, fill them all with refugees. Drive the entire population of the land behind walls then starve them out."

"You've gotten a hard edge to you, my friend," said Ariel, as she gently squeezed his shoulder.

"No, Lady Ariel, he's right," said Randall. "Look carefully at it. As we do this, people inside the walls will be cast out, the ones the Geni have no use for. We can gather them up, reinstall them in a village, help them survive. That way we create allies among the common people.

"We could send the odd wagon load of supplies into the city where they would be welcomed, and in so doing our allies could spy out the situation for us. We'd have to be extremely careful who we sent in, of course. Only those you trust completely, and yet who would be of no use as a man-at-arms."

"You mean you," grinned Drakkat. Randall just shrugged with a broad grin on his face.

"I don't like it," said Ariel, "but I can see the merit of it. Has anyone else got a better idea?" No one said anything so Ariel began to set up the table. "Here is Shotar, here lies Magdan, ..."

She went on to lay out the position of the cities. They determined that they needed five raiding groups. Each group would be about two hundred fifty strong. As soon as they gathered enough freed slaves to make up a troop they'd bring them to Fugitive.

Ariel wasn't happy that this would leave Fugitive somewhat unprotected, but Drakkat told her not to worry. "The Scratite will protect the town, Lady, besides, Lady Freida will be staying here, so between us, Fugitive will be safe enough."

"Freida? Will you not ride beside me, my sister?"

"Forgive me, Ariel, my queen, but I need to remain here at the forge. If I ride with you, the hate I bear the masters will take me over, and there will be no refugees to send into the cities."

Mearith reached over to lightly grip the woman's shoulder. "I understand, and I, for one, will be quite happy to have you here to defend Fugitive."

Ariel nodded. "All right, my sister, perhaps you're the wiser in this. I have only one request."

"Ariel?"

"Use your magic to make some armor."

"Sorry. I tried to learn to use it, but it constricts me, my movements."

Drakkat chuckled at that. "Did you see those men when she stripped off to her kilt then leaped into them? Most pissed themselves at the sheer fury of her attack. I think the princess Freida would make a fine Orc." She laughed and punched him on the arm.

The planning went on well into the night. In the end the warriors had been divided into the five groups. Ariel would lead one, Arlon another, Eline yet another while Tanis retained the Reavers. Mexah was to lead the last, while L'ark would remain to command the Elves left to defend Fugitive. Each of the five attack groups would have one mage in the party.

Once that was decided, Tanis recounted his methods of capturing the villages and towns. "I know this sounds a bit harsh, people," he said, "but it's something I learned from my master when I was quite young.

"He told his friends that to completely demoralize a slave and gain instant compliance, the command had to come swiftly, as a surprise, and harshly, leaving no room for resistance. This is what I do, sudden attack, harsh demands, to argue means death, leave no room for discussion, no bargaining, and no compassion."

"He's right," said Randall. "This is how you create refugees. You want demoralized people fleeing into the cities. Once they're cast out, then we can approach them with offers of help, food, and shelter. This is how we'll create allies."

"My concern lies with the slaves caught in the cities," said Ariel.

"Fear not, Ariel," grinned Randall. "The more slaves you set free the more valuable those left behind become, and as such, the more they will be treasured. My queen, you don't have the resources to fight an all-out war with the Geni. If you try, there will be far more loss of life than there will be this way."

"I see the sense in what you say, Randall," sighed Ariel. "They brought war to our house and were defeated. However, that battle cost us thirty-seven dead and nearly a hundred more injuries. We don't have the numbers to face that, and I wouldn't if there is any other way at all. No, this plan is the best we can hope for at this point."

"I do agree," said Mearith, "and these are tactics more natural to the Elves. Gormin, when the time comes to fight the cities, we may need the Dwarves."

"Mearith, I could comb the mountains for a year and not find enough warriors to make much of a difference."

"I don't want Dwarves for warriors," she grinned. "I want them to show me how to find the weaknesses, bring down the walls."

"Sappers? Oh aye, now, that we could do easily enough."

And so it went. When the next day dawned, the group leaders assembled their warriors and began to make plans, assign positions, so that the instant they had a newly freed slave that person would have a mentor. When Trelanth returned three weeks later, they were ready.

Since Eline hadn't been there for the planning, she was assigned her party from the warriors who had gone into the mountains with her as Second to a Thousand. They knew and trusted her. Trelanth was also assigned to her party so she would have the strongest mage. Ariel didn't need one.

Tanis and the Reavers had the longest stretch of roadway to cover so they went mounted on the wild ponies, Kern rode with them. Paden, the man who'd wanted to become a horse master, had learned a great deal, and was assigned to Ariel's party, as he seemed to have a greater affinity for the big war horses.

On the morning they all vanished into the forest, Drakkat, Horak, Marc, Freida, and L'ark stood atop the wall watching them go. It was Freida who spoke first. "Horak, I sense you think the queen might have forgotten something in all the excitement."

"Lady?"

"My friend, Ariel never forgets a promise. I'll wager L'ark has an errand to run at Shotar."

L'ark's laughter filled the air as he nodded. "Indeed I do, Lady Freida. Marc and I have a short trip to make to Shotar. Trelanth has already shown me the new path through the forest. We'll give the war parties two days to get well into their task then we'll go fetch your families. Kern left us enough horses for the journey."

"When we bring them here they'll have to live inside the walls until we finish building homes for all," said Marc. "That rebuilding will be a job for Humans, Orcs, and Dwarves. Elves aren't much good for building houses; they prefer to live under the trees."

"Laugh if you want, Marc," grinned L'ark, "but you need us to convince the forest to give up a few trees for timbers."

"There is that," grunted Drakkat. "So, if we're going to give Tanis time to create a distraction, we might as well do something useful. We've got houses to build and fields to tend. Let's get to it."

The Queen's Reavers

Tanis had promoted Kern as second, a move that surprised many of the warriors in his party. "If there are objections I'll hear them," said Tanis, as he made the announcement.

"Forgive me, Lord Tanis," said one Borni, as she stepped forward. "I do not object so much as I wish to understand the reasoning."

Tanis nodded. "All right, here's my reasoning. Each and every one of you is vital to this group; any one of you could fill the position and do it well. Of this I have no doubts at all.

"I chose Kern for several reasons. In the past, I've consulted him, among others, about attack plans, and each time he has shown me a better way. He seems to have a knack for this type of action. Also, as second, he will have to relay my commands to the rest of you as fast as possible. On horseback, there's no one faster.

"People, the Reavers are a mounted war party, and it's due to Kern we're able to strike so hard and fast in one place and the next day far away the same. The horses will obey him instantly. I know I can rely on your instant obedience, the horses not so much."

This made the Borni warrior laugh. "My Lord, your reasoning is without flaw as always. I bow to your greater wisdom."

"Lonna, I was serious when I said any of you could fill the post and I'd be blessed to have you." She smiled and nodded.

Kern limped forward. "People, I won't try to direct you in battle, for you have far more skill and wisdom in these matters. I'll remain slightly back, observing the action, bringing information to you that you can't see from where you are.

"Our Lord Commander always seems to get into the thick of the battle and loses sight of the overall action. That will be my task."

"And, as the second you need not go to Tanis for direction, but will be able to direct the battle with speed from horseback," smiled the warrior. "You are indeed the correct choice for second, Kern. I'm at peace with this.

"My Lord Tanis, I should point out that, as a Lord Commander, you need not explain your decisions to us."

"That will happen in battle situations, people," smiled Tanis, "but not in the preparation stages like this. We're a small group of elite warriors. We need to be sure of each other, and you need to understand and trust your leaders.

"So, are we settled on this matter?" There was a shout of general agreement from those gathered by the campfires.

The next morning, Tanis and Kern stood inside the tree line, observing the farming village below. "It appears our previous adventures have reached the ears of these good folk, my Lord."

"Looks like, all right. How many guards do you see?"

"I see a dozen slaves toiling at the soil with an equal number guarding them. Some are old men, others still boys, but all are watchful."

"I find it somewhat perplexing, Kern. With so many people there, if everybody worked the field the work would be swiftly done, and all could seek shade. This way they have to stand about in the heat while the slaves labor harder and suffer more than is needful."

"It's traditional," grinned the younger man. "My old master's wife used to complain that he stubbornly refused to change anything, even though a better way was right at hand. I think this is the same. These people were raised with slaves doing all the work, and that's how they believe it must be done."

"They can't all be that stubborn, can they? Perhaps I'll go ask them."

Kern chuckled at that. "My Lord Tanis, what do you suggest the rest of us should do while you're conferring with the farmers?"

"Those slaves look tired and thirsty, perhaps you could take them into the shade of the forest and find them some water."

"Now why didn't I think of that," laughed Kern, as he wheeled his horse and sped back to the rest of the war party.

Tanis rode down toward the nearest field where the slaves were hard at work under guard. As he neared, three men with drawn bows ran at him. "Hold where you are. Who are you? What is your business here?"

Tanis pulled his horse to a stop, his face well hidden by the hood he'd pulled forward. "My name is Tanis. I'm here to bring you news."

"News? What news? Speak up man."

"Lower your bow and I'd be happy to do so." Slowly, carefully, the men lowered the bows. "As I said, my name is Tanis and I bring news. The day is hot and the work of fields is hard. If all of you pitched in to help, the work would soon be done then all could seek shade and rest. Much more efficient this way."

"Don't be a fool man, if we did that the slaves would run away or the damned marauders would steal them."

"Marauders?"

"Runaway Elves. One of them thinks she's the High Born Queen remade. They've been raiding all up and down the king's highway, stealing slaves, murdering, and burning homes. They won't get our slaves, I can tell you. Let them come, we're ready for them."

"So, you're saying you've got another hundred men at arms hiding nearby?"

"What? No, we ... What is that?" he was pointing fearfully at the forest, which had just spilled out an army of mounted warriors.

Tanis turned in the saddle to look. "Looks like the Queen's Reavers to me. They'll probably kill the lot of you and burn everything they can find. I'd say you have only one chance to survive."

"What?" Tanis pushed back his hood. "You're an Elf. By all the gods, you're one of them."

"Good guess, my friend. Now, the day is hot and I'm getting cranky. Release the slaves to me, all of them, both these and those hidden within the walls. Do this and I'll let you live. Fight me and all will die. Choose quickly."

Fearfully the men dropped their bows as hundreds of mounted warriors raced across the fields towards them. The slaves were swept up onto horseback and carried off into the forest. The rest of the warriors drew bows. "Well, speak up. Bring out the rest of the slaves or my fighters will find them. If you care for the survival of your families, send them out."

The first man to have spoken dropped his bow and nodded. One of the others turned to the farmhouse and began shouting orders. Soon another five slaves were brought out to be swept up onto horseback and carried off. The families of the farmers were also led out, and then the buildings were looted before being set afire.

As the flames rose high the Elves gathered the horses and sped back into the forest. When they dismounted in a shady glade, one of the freed slaves was brought to Tanis.

To everyone's surprise he swept her into his arms and hugged her tightly. She eagerly returned the embrace as tears of joy ran down both their faces. "Oh sister, by all the gods, I dared not hope to find you alive after the way master beat and then sold you."

"Nor I you, my brother, my hero. I was lucky, it was a kind man who bought me. You, did I hear that man call you Lord Tanis?"

"Yes, you did. I lead these savage warriors," grinned Tanis. "Tell me, did we get all of you from that village?"

"You did. There have been so many tales of wild Elves burning and murdering. It's said you always strike at dawn, so we were forced to work in the heat of the day then locked in a hidden cellar beneath a barn at night. It was believed that if you didn't find any slaves you would let the people live."

"We always let them live," smiled Tanis. "We want them alive. We free the slaves, burn the homes, so they have to go to the cities for protection. Once there, they become a drain on the resources. Eventually they will be turned out again, and then we will help them rebuild, but only if they learn to live without slaves.

"Now, my beautiful sister, I will send you with a guardian who will take you to Fugitive where you will learn the ways of true Elves. I'll return there when the snows fall. But for the next few days you'll remain with me while the poison of the oshar leaves your body."

"Brother?"

"The oshar isn't a food, it's a poison. As it leaves your body you will awaken to your true nature as an Elf. I've experienced this myself, and I'll be right at your side as you awaken to your natural senses."

At this point, Kern rode towards them. "Brother, who is that man on the horse, and why am I so drawn to be near him. The strength of that desire is almost painful. Is it the compulsion?"

"By the look on his face I believe it is," grinned Tanis. "I hope you like horses."

His words were lost on her as her full attention was on the man who leaped nimbly to the ground then limped slowly towards them. She was completely unaware of rising to her feet and stepping into his path. As he neared she stepped into his arms and hugged him tightly.

With a wide grin of mischief, Tanis rose and spoke. "Kern, what's the meaning of this? Why have you taken my sister prisoner?"

"Forgive me, Lord Tanis, but it's I who has been taken prisoner." There was a great round of laughter at that.

"Kern, my brother-at-arms, when we were small this woman was named Dera, and so I name her again. Is it your desire to take her as your life companion?"

"It is that, my Lord. I beg you, grant permission or kill me now, for I cannot live without her."

"Dera is no longer a slave, Kern. This is her decision to make, not mine. What say you, my sister, will you bond with this mad horseman?"

"Yes, oh yes. Is this truly possible? Are we allowed to mate by our own choice?"

"You are, Dera," smiled Tanis, "and you've chosen wisely. This man is my second, and a personal friend to the queen. It appears that you'll have someone besides me to see you through the awakening. Keep her with you, Kern. Keep her safe."

He may as well have been talking to himself, for they had no eyes or ears except for each other.

The Forsaken

Saggit leaned heavily on his walking stick as he and Randall slipped into a group of refugees entering Shotar city. The entire group was stopped at the gate by armed Orcs. Three potential fighters were selected and allowed to pass through the gate, the rest were turned away.

Randall grinned as they made their way painfully towards the spreading mass of makeshift shelters outside the walls. They approached a number of Humans and Orcs gathered around a small fire. "Go away," snarled one female Orc. "We can't even feed our young, we have nothing to share."

"We do," said Saggit, keeping his voice down. He passed her a packet of dried fruits from his pack. "I seek news of the Tomac."

"They're gone with the men at arms, those who can fight. The rest of us are here, the families, elders and young. We were promised shelter and food if our men would fight."

"But instead, as soon as the troops entered the forest, you were cast out," he muttered. "The Geni have no honor. Speaking of honor, I need to find the mate of Kettar."

"I am that woman; the chieftain is my mate. What news do you have?"

Saggit saw the fear in her eyes. He reached to put a gentle hand on her shoulder. "There's no time now for what must be done. I swear there will be soon, for now it's best if you can remain silent."

Bracing herself for the worst, she squared her shoulders. "He's dead?"

"Yes. He challenged the chieftain of the Scratite Clan to a battle of honor. He fought well and the battle was long, but he was defeated. By common consent the Tomac have been adopted by the Scratite. Even now Horak sits in council with Drakkat, Chieftain of the Scratite Clan.

"We've come to take you, all of you, to them; we'll leave when darkness falls. Bring only what you can carry."

"And only those who can travel easily?"

"No, girl, bring them all. We have friends with food and horses nearby. Tell them to prepare, but quietly." She nodded then turned back to her children. She gave them the food he'd shared, then spoke softly to another woman. That one nodded then looked at Saggit before moving off to speak with another.

The chieftain's widow turned back to him. "So, they failed to capture the Elves?"

"They failed," he replied. "Only the Tomac survived, as they fought beside the Scratite and their new chieftain. The rest will not return, nor will they be found."

"So it's true, the Elf Queen has arisen to destroy her enemies."

"She has, and she will defeat the Geni."

"And the Scratite are allied with her?"

"They are. She and the chieftain have fought side by side many times."

"Is she as terrible in battle as the legends say?"

"She is, but it's her sister that frightens me," he chuckled. "That one is a blacksmith. The gods taught her how to make a special sword. When facing an enemy, no matter how many they are, she strips to her kilt and attacks. Ah, she's a wonder to behold.

"Now, let's speak of another matter. You were chieftain's mate, but he was slain in a challenge of honor. Where does that leave you, in clan status?"

She clenched her jaw tightly. "It will leave me and my children beggars, for the clan has little money, and no farms or resources. The families of the survivors will claim what little there is."

"There is another possible path," he said softly. "This staff is a disguise only, for although old, I'm still strong. My name is Saggit. I'm the lore speaker of Scratite Clan, my brother is the chieftain. As my mate, you would have status, food and shelter, as well as allies to defend you and your young. If you agree I will claim them as my own."

"You would do this? Truly?" He nodded. "Why?"

"Because he fought with honor. There's damn little honor left in the world these days. My mate and her children were killed in a sea rover raid long ago, and I have not claimed another since. Kettar was an honorable man, and I expect his children will carry that with them. They should have the chance to do so, not as beggars looking for scraps, but as free folk, living free on the land.

"Take your time, think it over. A better option may present itself."

"It won't," she sighed, allowing her shoulder to slump. "I accept you, if you swear not to harm my children."

"I swear on my honor, and that of my clan, to do my best for you and your children." He held out his huge hand and she placed hers in it.

"What is your wish, my mate?"

"Gather the others, keep secret what I've told you until we are well away from these accursed walls. We'll leave in the night and be far away when the sun next touches the lands. There we will rest, and all will eat their fill.

"We have Human allies nearby who will meet us with horses and supplies. Trust me, by this time on the morrow you will have seen the last of these walls."

"That will please me greatly. Saggit."

"Yes?"

"You new mate is called Kreen."

He grinned as he gave her hand a squeeze. "It's a good name, a strong name, for a fine woman. Truly, I'm a lucky man."

She smiled and turned away to seek the others. It hurt to have lost her mate, for he'd been good to her, but fortune had smiled on her again. This old Orc was far more than he seemed. No matter where he took her it would be better than here, groveling before the Geni for food scraps to give her children.

Saggit led his new mate and the families of the Tomac clan away from the walls of Shotar and into the forest where Marc met them with food and horses. As they lay down to rest with full bellies for the first time in months, far away, Tanis stood gazing out at a village in the valley below.

"My Lord Tanis, the scouts have returned."

"Good," he nodded. "Bring them to my fire, Kern and Ethor as well."

"Sir." The Elf hurried away as Tanis turned back and made his way to the small campfire. They'd made camp early that day, and he'd been lost in thought ever since.

"I can hear the sounds of battle from here," grinned Ethor, as he sat to the fire. Tanis quirked an eyebrow at him. "Your thoughts, Lord Tanis, they are clearly at war with one another." Kern chuckled at that as he and Dera joined them.

"You have the truth of it, Ethor, my friend. Help me now, all of you. Below us, out in the open fields by the king's road, lies a large village of Humans and Orcs. It's the last one, the only one now standing between Shotar and Magdan.

"Before we left Fugitive, Queen Ariel told me of her desire for these people. She would like me to create a truce with this one, create a place of sanctuary for Humans and Orcs, if you will."

"Oh?"

"Yes. She believes we can live in peace with them, trading back and forth as free folk all."

Ethor nodded, absorbing the information. "Do you disagree with her reasoning?"

"My mind, not so much, but my heart, yes. May the queen forgive me for this, but she was raised in relative luxury compared to the rest of us. I remember my former life all too well, as do at least half the warriors in the Reavers. In truth, my every instinct says kill the lot of them, and I'm sure it's the same for the rest of the Bornani.

"So, what think you? If I do this as the queen desires, will I have a mutiny on my hands? Should I make a feeble attempt, but taunt them into attacking me anyway then burn them out? Give me your thoughts on this."

"Tanis, you cannot disobey the queen," grinned Ethor. "I know you too well for that. No matter what she asks of you, you'll do it, we all will. What is it you truly want from us?"

"I don't know," he sighed, "your strength, your trust, your support, some encouragement maybe."

"You have that, always," replied Kern. "Tanis, my brother, my Lord, speak to the Reavers all. Right now, you wrestle with doubts and fear."

"He's right," agreed Ethor. "These things serve the desires of the Geni. Speak to the Reavers, destroy the weapons of the enemy. Help the queen create the new world she's envisioned for us all."

"You must be strong, Tanis," Dera said softly, as she gripped his hand. "The others draw their strength and courage from you. If you explain to them what we do, and why, they will support you fully in this. Tanis, when you first brought me out you told me you do what you do for the queen, for the people."

"For the queen, for the people?"

"Yes, my Lord Tanis," she grinned, "for the queen, for the people."

He returned her warm smile then rose to his feet. "Well then, shall we be about it? Ethor, can you enhance my voice so all can hear?"

"Speak, my Lord, and it shall be as you desire," grinned the mage.

Tanis faced the encampment of his warriors. "Hear me, Queen's Reavers. We have a new task now. It is the desire of the queen that we make allies of the people in that village below. It is the desire of Her Majesty to drive the Geni from these lands, yet to share the lands with Humans, Orcs, Dwarves, and any others we may find who will be willing to live in peace with us.

"This will be a much harder task than we have faced before, and I will ask things of you that may be quite distasteful to you. As always, we'll discuss this now before we approach the coming battle.

"First, I want scouts well out in both directions, some towards Shotar, and others towards Magdan. If a man-at-arms is on that road, I want to know about it a full day before he reaches this place.

"Second, and here's the hard part, I need a number of the Bornani who have worked the farms before, to comb through the forest and gather up what livestock they find running free. Bring it all here to the village." There were some grumbles at that.

"I can hear your objections, and I confess I do agree with you here, but this must be done. However, I won't make it an order. I want volunteers. Who among you will help me make the queen's desire a reality?"

No one moved or spoke for a moment, then an older man stepped forward. "My Lord, I'll volunteer, but I would ask a favor, if I may?"

"Ask."

"My Lord, when I was taken from the farm by L'ark, I was brought to the Borni who taught me the ways of the forest and of combat. Sir, I'd like to return the favor now. Send a Borni warrior with me and I'll teach him the ways of swine herding."

There was a round of laughter at that. "So be it," grinned Tanis. "Who among the Borni will volunteer for these lessons?"

"I will," said a tall woman, as she stepped forward. "I'm always ready to learn new things."

"I'll go," said another warrior, "if I get Borni to work with me."

"Done then," said Tanis. "Any more?" Two more Bornani stepped forward and, with heads shaking ruefully, A Borni warrior stepped up beside each one.

"I can't begin to tell you how proud I am to serve with the Queen's Reavers," said Tanis. "When it comes time to work the fields and build homes, I'll work beside any who are willing to teach me. Rest well, my friends. In the morning, the scouts will set out, the next day we'll make contact."

Two days later the people of the village rose at dawn to find a lone horseman sitting atop his mount in the village square. A woman with silvery hair came out to meet him. "We've been expecting you, Elf, but you're wasting your time here."

Tanis pushed back his hood and smiled. "How is it that my time is wasted, good woman? Are you headman here?"

"I am that," she replied. "You're wasting your time because those thieving bastards from Magdan came and pillaged the place already. They took the slaves, horses, whatever money, and valuables they could find, as well as most of the winter's food supply. Go ahead, look for yourself."

"Don't mind if I do," he replied. At a signal from his hand Elvish warriors appeared from behind buildings and, with drawn weapons, searched the village.

"All is as she said, my Lord Tanis," reported one man, as they finished their search. "There are no slaves to be found, and precious little else."

Tanis nodded and thanked him before turning back to the old woman. "I see by the folk gathering that they also took every man able to wield a sword with them as well."

"They did."

Tanis gazed at her for a long moment, taking her measure. He grinned to see her doing the same. There was no fear in her, just a controlled defiance. He liked that. "My name's Tanis, and I'm here to represent the wishes of Queen Ariel."

He held out his hand and she gazed at it for a moment. "Grace, headman for this village," she replied, gripping his hand for a moment.

"All right, Grace. Do you speak for these people, and will they comply with any bargain you make?"

"I can and they will or get their useless carcasses out of Argar. What's on your mind, Lord Tanis?"

In that single moment, she won his friendship forever. She'd spoken his name with genuine respect. "Tanis will do fine, Grace. Listen now, here's the bargain the queen offers. Swear to me you will no longer make use of slaves in any fashion for any reason. In return we'll leave your village unharmed. Moreover, we'll help with the fields and see if we can return some livestock to you.

"In future, Elves are to be welcomed in Argar as free folk. We'll trade fairly with you whenever we come. The folk of Argar will be our allies and under our protection as much as possible."

"As much as possible?"

"Sadly, Grace, we can't leave a thousand warriors here to garrison the place, but we will be patrolling the forests and the roads. You may have noticed a lack of robbers and brigands along the roadway this season."

"We had noticed that," she grinned. "The only brigands now are from Magdan."

"Yes, well, perhaps I can do something about that as well, at least for now."

"Oh? I'm not so certain. They'll be back before the snows fall to steal whatever we have left; they need to feed their army through the winter."

"I know," he grinned, "and I'd be happier if that army went hungry. Ethor."

A man in a long mage robe approached. "My Lord?"

"Is there anyone from Magdan watching this section of the road?"

"There is, at least they're trying. They're having a bit of difficulty at the moment."

Tanis chuckled at that. "Could you show them something interesting?"

"What do you have in mind?"

"Show them a thousand Elvish warriors on the road and this village burning."

"With extreme pleasure, my Lord. I'll just find a shady spot to work." As he walked away Tanis signaled and a dozen warriors followed the mage and stood guard while he performed his task.

Tanis turned back to the woman. "Now then, Grace, do we have a bargain?"

"If you're serious, yes, of course," she replied, and shook the hand he offered. "Why? Why do this?"

"Because the queen wants all people to live in harmony. Slavery must end, forever, but those who put us in chains are long since dead from the march of time. She dreams of a better world, Grace. Help us, help her, to make that happen. All you have to do is accept Elves as free folk, free and equal people."

"Done, Tanis. If all we have to do to keep our people alive is learn to live without slaves, then that's what we'll do. Too few of us ever had the money to buy one anyway. This will be less of a hardship than you think."

"Really?"

"Well, I know there'll be people who are hardheaded, and others who'll be determined to feel and act superior, but with time we should get there. Your queen understands this won't happen overnight, right?"

"She doesn't expect it to be easy, Grace, but she does expect it to happen. She will make it happen. I've seen a taste of the power she can wield, and the mages tell me they've never seen anything like it, not even in elder days in the war of the Geni. You've chosen wisely, my friend."

"I'll believe that when I see an Elf warrior bringing livestock out of the forest."

He just grinned at her. "Wait a few days. It'll happen. Now, tell me, what work needs to be done this day?"

Three days later they stood side by side, Tanis with blisters on his hands, watching the Elves herd a number of swine and cattle out of the forest and across the fields. Behind them Kern and Dera brought several big draft horses with them.

Within a week Argar looked quite prosperous. The fields had been harvested, the storehouses filled, hay and grain in the barns for the stock, and all seemed well.

Once again, Tanis was deep in thought, this time in the village inn. "What's tormenting you this time, my Lord," asked Ethor as he joined him. "Have we not succeeded as we intended to do?"

"We have, but to what end?"

"Tanis?"

"What now, Ethor my friend, do we ride away and leave these folk to their fate?"

Grace and a few others perked up at that. Kern as well. "What do you think, my brother," he grinned, "should we send Magdan a message?"

"I'd like to do a bit more," Tanis replied. "Is there no word from the scouts?"

"None. All is quiet."

"That can't last. I can feel the snows in the air. Both Shotar and Magdan will be sending out armed men to forage for food before the snows cover the land. They'll bring slaves and wagons, gather what's not already been pulled from the ground, and send out hunters as well."

"What can we do, my Lord? It's many days of hard travel between Magdan and Shotar. We can't be everywhere at once."

"Actually, that's exactly what I have in mind," grinned Tanis. "Kern, we will have to work very differently, you and I."

"Tanis, what are you planning here?" asked Kern, suddenly wary. "I'm a horseman, just a horseman, and already you've pushed me into the position of command as your second. What are you going to do to me now?"

"I'll take half the Reavers towards Magdan," replied Tanis, "as that's where Argar is expecting trouble from. You take the rest and head for Shotar. Don't bother going through the forest, use the road, it's faster."

"So, I'm to capture Shotar with a hundred Reavers?" This made Tanis laugh and brought a smile to every face.

"No, you're looking for something else. As soon as you get close to the city, or if you see men-at-arms, flee into the forest. You're looking for hunters. No hunter entering the forest is to return. The cities must know the forest is our realm.

"Also, if you see men-at-arms with slaves, rescue them if you can. Kern, swear to me you'll take no risks, just eliminate the hunters, and do what you can with the rest. Send them back behind city walls empty-handed if you can but take no chances.

"Torment the men-at-arms but elude them. We want them alive and in the city through the winter. The more of them there are the faster their food stores will be depleted."

Kern was thoughtful, nodded his head slowly as he absorbed the plan. Slowly a grin crossed his face. "Torment them. Tell me, how fast can a big horse, carrying a heavy saddle, a man twice my size with armor and weapons, run? Fast enough to catch an Elf on a Narthwood forest pony, do you think?"

"Kern, no chances, you hear me?"

"Yes, my Lord Tanis. Destroy the hunters and avoid the men-at-arms. What should I do if a few men at arms chase me into the forest?"

"Kern, get out of here and choose your people. Dera, keep a rein on him, will you?"

"Yes, dear brother, I'll keep him safe."

She was grinning as she followed Kern through the door. Tanis just shook his head and followed. In mere moments, Kern and a hundred more were mounted. "Kern."

"Yes, my Lord, no chances. Where and when shall we meet?"

"When the snows fall, return here to Argar. We'll make new plans from there." Kern saluted and rode away with his warriors close behind.

Tanis turned back towards those who remained. "Lonna, you're my new second. Prepare, we ride toward Magdan within the hour. Ethor, tell me truly, how far can you shield a man from prying eyes?"

"Tanis?"

"If you remain here can you keep the Geni from seeing us as well as Kern?"

"Are you serious?"

"Ethor, if you can't, go with Kern, keep him safe."

The mage sighed and let his shoulders slump. "I can probably do it from here, but it'll be a serious stretch. I won't be much use for anything else, just eat sleep, and project, and I won't be able to keep it up for long."

"If it's a bad idea you can say no, old friend."

"No, Tanis, I'll do it. Probably do me good to stretch my abilities a bit."

Tanis gave him a pat on the shoulder. "Give Kern five days then begin."

"And you?"

"Five days as well. Look for me near the walls of Magdan." With that he strode away.

That night, as they camped at the edge of the forest, Tanis spoke to his warriors. "Tell me, Borni, who among you has fought the Geni in times past?"

"We all have," replied Lonna.

"All right then, what are we facing and how do we combat it?"

"My Lord, in such battles things happen fast. The Geni will throw distraction spells at us, weakness spells to slow us down, and more."

"How do we fight this?"

"The distraction spells can be overcome by force of will. Once the enemy is engaged, focus completely on that, ignore all else, all sound, all visions, stay focused on defeating the enemy before you.

"The weakness spells are another matter. There are counter spells, and we all know them, but we haven't had use for them since that war that drove us from this world."

"You must teach us these counter spells, and how to use them. We begin now for there's no time to lose," replied Tanis. Seven days later, they saw the walls of Magdan. Two hundred men at arms rode out to meet them.

A shout of alarm sounded as the lead rider sighted the Elves. A war horn shattered the morning air and the thunder of pounding hooves followed the sound. The mounted men began to spread out as they charged toward the oncoming Elves.

To the shock of the charging warriors, the Elvish riders split apart into two groups that swept wide, their lighter and faster ponies easily avoiding the heavier war horses. Arrows flew from Elvish bows and several riders fell from their saddles.

As they swept past, the Elves turned and rode for the forest on either side of the highway. The commander of Magdan's forces tried to call the men back, but to no avail.

Tanis grinned as he looked over his shoulder. Once they had the riders well spread out they swung around again and went back at the few who had remained with the commander. Those broke and fled towards the safety of the city walls, leaving the two dozen slaves and the wagons unguarded.

The Elvish riders swung around again, charging at the riders left in the field, then racing past just out of reach. The bows sang and more riders fell. Again, the men-at-arms gave chase to no avail. Tanis could hear the voices all around him and feel the resolve and strength leave his body, but he gritted his teeth and fought it, focusing on the plan, muttering the counter chant over and over.

At length, he stopped to face the men-at-arms across a wide span of open field. His pony was sweating and breathing deeply, but the war horses were exhausted; so were the armed riders. Tanis watched as they slowly regrouped, then he alone approached them.

"Ho there, men of Magdan."

"What do you want, Elf?"

"My name is Tanis, and I can see that most of you would make better farmers than warriors."

"Come closer, slave, and I'll show you what kind of warrior I am," shouted an Orc.

Tanis ignored him. "Hear me, you men. There is a village named Argar a few days hence. Are any of you from that town?"

"Why do you ask?" came a different voice.

"I ask because I've been there. Their homes are warm, and the storehouses are full. Grace says the men are welcome to return as long as they live by the new rules."

"New rules? What new rules?"

"No slaves," replied Tanis. "Argar has allied with the Elf Queen, and is now under her protection. If you're willing to do your own work you're welcome to return. The village still stands, and the storehouses are full.

"Think about this, you're farmers and tradesmen, not warriors. We could have killed the lot of you easily this day, but we didn't. Just throw down your weapons and ride out for Argar, we won't hinder you."

It took a moment, then one man threw down his sword and slowly rode away, stripping off and tossing aside his armor as he went. The

Elves moved aside to let him pass. Another joined him and then another. In all, a dozen men rode away on tired horses.

When no more moved Tanis spoke again. "The rest of you look carefully, half your numbers are dead or deserted, the wagons and slaves are gone as well, and none rode from Magdan to come to your aid. It's well they didn't, for there are thousands more Elves in the nearby forest.

"The forests are ours, and now so are the roadways. The only place of safety left to you is within the city walls. Go there now, I won't offer again."

Cursing, yet defeated, they rode slowly back to the city and disappeared through the gates, even though their numbers exceeded that of the Elves. Across the road, the other riders were also turning back while a few headed for Argar.

As they did, the chattering voices and the weakness suddenly disappeared, and Tanis sighed with relief. "Damn, this could have actually been fun if Ethor or Trelanth were here. Damned Geni magic anyway." He signaled and his warriors joined him at the road. They followed the men and wagons.

That night all camped together. The men were nervous amid the war band of Elves, and Tanis played on that. He let them watch as he removed the slave collars from the newly freed, then he let them listen as he explained about the oshar. This confused the men as well as the Elves.

One of the newly freed was trying to get his attention. "Yes, my brother?"

"Sir, forgive me, but I remember you. I heard one of the Borni call you Lord Tanis. Are you our new owner?"

"You have no owner now, my brother, nor will you ever again. Yes, I am called Lord Tanis. The title of Lord Commander is given to a man or woman who commands a thousand warriors. Those men are in the forest now, watching Magdan. As soon as the Geni sends more men at arms to recapture you, they will sack the city, kill all within the walls, then burn it to the ground."

Lonna had been watching one of the men and, with lightning speed she seized the man and stripped the fetish from his hand. She threw it in the fire where they heard a scream as the flames not only destroyed the fetish, but burned the watching Geni mage as well. The man was thrown to the ground at Tanis' feet.

"Do any of more of you have one of these things?" asked Tanis. "If you do, burn it now or face a painful death when we find it."

"There are no more, Elf," said one of the men. "He had the only one."

A sword appeared at the man's throat. "The man's title is Lord Commander, and you will use that title when you speak to him or die where you stand," growled one of the Bornani who had been brought out of Magdan by the queen herself. "We're not your slaves anymore, and you will put some respect in your voice, or we'll do it for you." The man swallowed hard and flinched away.

"Hear me, good men," said Tanis, "the times have changed. There are no more slaves, and yet we aren't enemies, we're allies. The Geni are the enemy. All we ask of you is to be respectful to us as we will be to you. We're allies, equals, sharing the world, living together in harmony. In Argar you will find the truth of this. Grace is headman there, and she has embraced the new ways.

"Having said that, if you feel you can't live with Elves walking about freely, speaking freely, trading freely as equals, you may turn back to Magdan." He turned to the man who'd had the speaking fetish. "Get out of here and return to grovel at your master's feet. Go now or be killed where you stand." The man fled the camp with two Elves following closely. He went alone.

Tanis turned back to the others. "Tell me now, how do things fare in Magdan?"

"Things are not well in the city, Lord Commander," replied the man the Bornani had chastised. "I was only there a short time, but it's easy to see. Some of the townsfolk told me tales of poverty and hunger. After the queen took away the slaves, more were brought in, but only enough to serve a few of the wealthy.

"The Geni overlord made certain he got his share first and the rest paid dearly for those who remained. Since you've been raiding and pillaging up and down the highway things have gotten worse. Food is tightly rationed among the poorer people. Men-at-arms get two meals a day, the rest but one."

"And the wealthy?"

"Eat their fill as always, Lord Commander."

Tanis grinned at that. "So, now that we've freed more of the slaves, the wealthy will be forced to hire servants from the poorer masses." He grinned and turned his attention to the newly freed Elves. "Tell me, my brothers and sisters, who among you knows of the storehouses in Magdan?"

"I do," said an older Elf. "It was I who kept the records, and, by my master's commands, doled out the food stores. I was sent out with the men-at-arms to show them which things to bring back. You know, what was in short supply."

"I see. Tell me of the food stores, will they last the winter?"

"Doubtful, Lord Commander. They might if the wealthy would ration themselves or manage to eat poorer foods, but they won't. The delicacies will be gone well before midwinter. The rest will surely be gone before the snows melt in spring.

"My Lord, what is to become of us now?"

"First, you will pass through the awakening as the oshar poison leaves your body. This is a truly magical experience, and we will travel slowly to allow you to enjoy it. Once we reach Argar, I'll send you on to Fugitive where others will help you learn the old language as well as woodcraft and skills at arms.

"From there, you will be taken across the mountains to Elfhome. There you will rest and learn many new things before deciding on your life's path."

"We must decide?"

"Yes. Once you see some of the many possibilities, you will be better able to make a choice that pleases you. Bort!"

A warrior rose and approached. "My Lord?"

"Join us for a moment. Now then, Bort was brought out of Magdan by the queen herself. Bort, tell our new brother of your adventures."

The Elf grinned. "It was a frightening and exciting time, my friend. I'd been whipped and sent to the auctions. The queen appeared and captured the city, then led us all out into the forest. The first night we were camped in the trees I felt it, the compulsion.

"I was terrified, as you can well imagine. Then I saw her, a Borni warrior, searching through the newly freed, looking for something, someone. Her eyes met mine and she came to me, took me to her campfire, and we've been together since that time.

"I was given the choice of what my life course might be, and I'll admit I considered remaining in Elfhome to study, but Kela's a warrior and a free spirit of the forest. She offered to stay with me in Elfhome, but I couldn't do that to her. We joined the Queen's Reavers under the command of Lord Tanis and here I am."

"Regrets, Bort?"

"None, my Lord Tanis. None at all. I spend my days free in the forest, I am carried about by that magical pony, and I'm ever beside my love, she who chose me and allowed me to choose for myself. I regret nothing."

"Thanks, Bort," smiled Tanis. "Go back now before she starts throwing stones at me for keeping you so long." The man laughed as he rose and left to rejoin his mate and their companions at their fire.

Tanis returned his attention the newly freed. "You see, my friends. You, too, will have the freedom to choose your own path. The Warriors who defend the forest are the Borni out of our legends. The others were all slaves even as you were.

"We're the descendants of the High Born Elves. We are the Bornani, the Children of the Forest. Never again will we build magical cities, but we will run through the forest as our ancestors did in ages gone by. There are many Bornani in this party. Speak with them if you wish, they will be more than happy to answer all your questions." With that, he rose then sought his blanket.

FAR AWAY IN ELFHOME the king paced slowly. His queen approached and took his arm. "My Lord King, Evan, what troubles you so?"

He sighed and kissed her cheek. "It's Ariel. We haven't heard a thing from her since the spring, and today the first dusting of snow has fallen. I feel the forest growing tired, needing rest, and ..."

"Call Orin to us. Surely, he can give us some insight into the affairs of the world. Evan, if anything had happened to the queen surely we would have known before now."

"My beautiful Belia, how is it that one so very young is so very old in wisdom? However did I manage without you?"

Blushing shyly, she kissed his cheek. "Call Orin to us now, let him set your mind at ease."

He signaled and a guardsman came instantly to him, then hurried away in search of the royal mage. He soon returned with the mage at his side. "You sent for me, my King?"

"I did, Orin. I confess to being somewhat troubled at the lack of news from our queen."

"Have you tried the talking stone, Sire?"

"All to no avail, I fear," sighed the king. "Queen Ariel is becoming far too much like Mearith."

The mage grinned as he spoke. "I can tell you, Sire, there has been a battle at Fugitive. Perhaps Queen Ariel lost the stone during that encounter."

"A battle? The queen?"

"She's fine, Sire. I confess I was exploring their whereabouts when you sent for me. It seems they have changed their tactics somewhat. I saw the queen and her lady companion leading barely two hundred warriors. Still other parties of equal size harry the countryside, driving all to seek safety in the cities.

"Sire, I believe the tactics that the Geni used against us so long ago are now being used against them. Perhaps we'll learn more when the Bornani arrive."

"The Bornani?"

"They've just passed the second waystation, Sire. They'll reach Narthwood in a matter of days and Elfhome within a moon cycle. L'mak is leading the Borni escort, he will surely have much news to impart to us.

"The snows are a half moon cycle away from the warm lands as yet. However, I did manage to connect with Trelanth for a short moment. She tells me the queen will remain at Fugitive for the winter. She wants to be near the gates of Shotar when the snows begin to melt."

"And as usual they leave me in the dark," grumbled the king. "Ah well, that's not my task. Are the new homes built for the Bornani?"

"They are ready and waiting, Sire. We've made amazing strides this year, and the ancient forest has been generous. The people will be well nurtured here in Narthwood, Sire. The new Bornani have teachers and families waiting to adopt them as soon as they arrive.

"The homes are built, the forges are built, the store houses are full, and enough firewood for a long winter has been gathered. The scholars have already begun construction of a new learning center. The forest showed us another cavern with plenty of room to store the scrolls and such."

"So all is well?"

"All is well, Sire."

"I'm worrying for nothing?"

"Perhaps the Lady Belia might offer a different subject to occupy your mind, Sire."

"Excuse me?"

"Sire, I do believe the queen to be with child."

"What??? Belia?"

"I was uncertain as this will be my first, and it is early days yet, but I think Orin has the right of it."

Evanseth gave a shout of delight and swept her into his arms, swinging her around and around while she shrieked with laughter. All was well in the north.

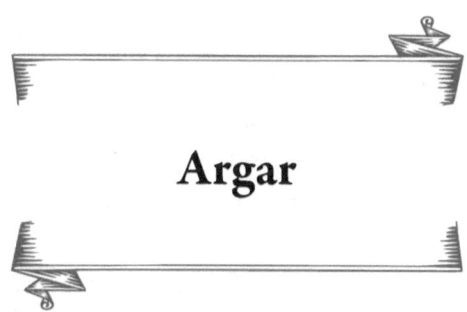

Argar

While Evanseth celebrated, fussed over, and doted on, his beloved queen Belia, things were not so smooth in the south. The raiding parties of the Elves had turned up nearly five hundred more slaves to be set free. The raids had been swift and efficient, driving nearly the entire population of the lands behind the walls of the five major cities.

Villages had been burned, towns burned, slaves freed, money taken, livestock driven off, and horses stolen. The people fled in terror, but in each section, a village was spared the fire. The slaves were removed, the masters driven off.

Those who were willing to live the new way as allies of the Elves were aided. The Elves helped with the harvest, brought back much of the livestock, and helped to fill the storehouses. Two hundred Elvish warriors remained behind in the forest to safeguard the new allies in case the cities tried to raid them.

Ariel returned to Fugitive with barely a handful of warriors and a few dozen freed slaves from the last town she'd made an ally. Snow was falling as she arrived to a wild welcome. One week later, in a lightly falling snow, Eline returned, the last of the war leaders.

Riding with her was a man Ariel had brought out of Magdan. He informed her that Lord Tanis would not return, although he had been extremely successful.

She sat quietly listening as Eline recounted her adventures. "Eline, you've done well, and I'm pleased with the results. Know that we have all met with success, for the enemy wasn't expecting these tactics. Gather the other leaders and return to me."

The girl was up and gone in a heartbeat. She soon returned with Arlon and the rest. "All right, good people. We were successful, more than, and that has created another problem that I hadn't planned for."

"Lady?"

"L'mak took the Bornani to Elfhome, but here we are with almost another two hundred more and it's too late to risk the mountains. The snows will already be deep up there."

"We can keep them here, Lady," said Trelanth. "The storehouses are full and the forests are welcoming. We have already begun to teach them the ways of the forest. We can keep them here safely and send them over the mountains in the spring."

"Sadly, that will put a terrible strain on our resources," said Marc. "We can do it, my queen, but I'll be praying for a mild winter."

"Aye, that's the truth of it," agreed Gormin. "We've already got a hundred new Orcs in the valley."

"Please, people," sighed Ariel, "show me another path. I'm completely open to hearing suggestions, no matter how unlikely. We have to care for these people as we promised. What can we do?"

It was Ethor who spoke up. "Lady, the year is early yet, and the snows aren't impassible, even in the high passes. "Let me take a hundred into the mountains. I'll take the strongest, and leave half of them at the first waystation. It's well stocked and they'll pass the winter easily enough.

"I'll drop the rest of them at the second waystation then return to you here."

No one spoke as Ariel mulled this over in her mind. It was clear she didn't like it, but she saw no better way. "Mearith?"

"It's the best solution of a bad lot, Ariel. The only other option we have is to take them back to the towns where we found them. They'd be too vulnerable there."

"You're right," sighed Ariel. "There is no better way. I'll lead them myself."

"No, my delight," Mearith said gently as she lightly patted Ariel's hand. "You must remain here if the overall plan is to succeed. You know what we have to do this winter."

"You're going to make me travel the length and breadth of the land in winter, aren't you?"

"My delight, I..."

"Oh no, you're coming with me. If I'm freezing my buttocks off all winter, then so are you. All right, I see no better way. Anyone else?" No one spoke. "Very well then, Eline, gather a hundred warriors from our slim ranks and assist Ethor on his journey." Eline bowed and left the inn to gather her troops.

Ariel turned to Drakkat. "My brother-in-arms, this will leave the defenses of Fugitive somewhat depleted."

"Don't worry, my queen," he grinned. "The Scratite will defend Fugitive for you. See to your new people."

"I suppose you'll want to remain here," said Ariel, as she turned to Freida.

"Forgive me, my queen, my sister, but I must remain at the forge. Besides, without me who knows what trouble Drakkat would get into." Laughing, she ducked away from the playful swipe he took at her.

"So be it," declared Ariel. "Marc, try to keep those two out of trouble, will you."

"I'll do my best, my queen," he grinned, "but you set me a hard task indeed. When will you leave?"

"We will all depart in the morning. Ethor, perhaps the storehouses could spare a sack or two of root vegetables, if you get my meaning."

"I do, my queen. Thank you." With that he rose and left the inn.

"Giving him the means to make allies?" asked Mearith.

"Yes, dear heart, having those Coti people as allies in the mountains will mean far fewer warriors needed to escort the new Bornani."

"So, we leave in the morning?"

"We do. I want to see what Tanis is up to. He didn't return to me, so I expect he's got something on the go that will benefit us all."

"That young lad is a treasure, all right," agreed Mearith. "I wonder what he's up to?"

The next morning the snow had stopped falling. Ethor led his two hundred plus towards the mountains while Ariel, Mearith, and the royal guard headed out to find Tanis.

TANIS SAT STARING AT the table the folks of Argar had begun calling the war table. Tanis had claimed that one and slowly built up a map of the roadway between Magdan and Shotar. He worked from memory and that of his people. As he mulled over yet another adjustment, he heard horses outside.

Thinking it was Kern returning he rose from the bench, but it was Ariel's voice he heard. "Ho there, travelers. What seek you in Argar?" That was the alert signal that mounted riders were in the village.

"My name is Ariel," replied the rider. "I'm queen of all Elves and I seek a deserter from my armies. His name is Tanis." She laughed with glee and leaped down from her horse as, wide-eyed, he emerged from the inn and dropped to one knee.

"My queen, I ..."

"Rise, dear friend," grinned Ariel. "Poor Tanis. He never can tell when I'm teasing." She raised him then stepped into his arms and gave him a gentle hug. "Tanis, I see very few Elves near this town, tell me what happened."

"With pleasure, my queen," he smiled as he held open the door for her. "Grace, could someone see to the horses?"

"Consider it done," she replied. A moment later, she returned to the inn to find Tanis showing the queen his war table, explaining how and where he had fought and succeeded.

"The Bornani you set free arrived in Fugitive and are now well into the mountains with Ethor and Eline. They will winter at the waystations," said Mearith.

"Tanis, it saddens me to know you've lost so many of the Reavers," sighed Ariel. "I grieve at your loss."

"Lady, the Reavers aren't lost. They're on their way back to us now. When first I heard your horses, I thought it might be Kern and Dera returning. Lady, I confess I remained here for good reason. Did Ethor not deliver my message?"

"He did, Tanis. He said you remained to defend this town, but do you truly expect trouble in the depths of winter?"

"Late in the winter or very early spring, yes. My queen, the riders from Magdan have come out twice already. Once before we arrived, and again after we'd made our alliance. The first time they took all the men and women capable of wielding a sword, plus as much food stores as they could steal.

"The second time they came at harvest time with two hundred men-at-arms, three wagons, and a dozen slaves. We defeated them and sent them back without the wagons or slaves.

"My queen, I do expect them to send more through the snows. According to the slaves we freed they will be desperate for food supplies by mid-winter."

"Then I will return to Fugitive and send you as many warriors as can be spared," said Ariel.

"Lady, no, that's not necessary," he replied. "My queen, the reason you found so few Elves here is they are all here." He gestured at the road marked on the table. "We've been more successful than expected. Already Shotar is pushing the weak out the gates, as is Magdan.

"The Reavers have been foraging through the fields we forced the people to abandon. We gather what food we can to deny it to the cities. Deep in the night we distribute it to those huddled outside the city walls.

"We also gather what few there who will be strong enough to work the farms, elder tradsfolk, smiths, tailors, leather workers, etc., and bring them here. Lady, we're filling up this town with allies. We also gathered a few able-bodied farmers from the men at arms we defeated at Magdan.

"Sadly, I had to send Ethor to Fugitive and thus have no mage, so the Geni are fully aware of what we do. However, we do have scouts all along the road, and everybody practices daily the counter spells."

"Counter spells?"

"Yes, Lady. The Geni attack with distraction and weakness spells, but the Borni have fought this before. They taught us the counter spells. It's a lot harder without the mage, but we've managed so far."

Ariel suddenly began to pace. "So, they're watching, are they. Well then, I'll give them something to see." She stopped still and closed her eyes. A glow of white light appeared and surrounded her. She brought her hands together and waist level, palms up and a stronger light appeared there.

Suddenly they could see into that light she held in her hands. In it they saw armed and mounted Elves, thousands of them emerging from the forest in a never-ending flow. The Elves split into two groups, one heading toward Magdan and the other toward Shotar.

The flow of Elvish warriors went on for some time, then Ariel raised her arms high and spoke in an other-worldly voice. "I see you, Geni, even as you see me. Know this, I will come for you when the snows leave the lands. Your only chance to survive is to send out all the Elves beyond your walls.

"Don't make me come get them, for if I do, not one Geni will survive. I have returned for my people, and I have returned to destroy those who invaded my lands." As she spoke the last, the light in her hands exploded into blinding light.

"There now," said Ariel. "They won't be able to see a thing for many days. They now know thousands of warriors are on the roads, and when next they look they won't see them. They'll believe they're in the forests, waiting. I'll leave Trelanth with you until I can get another mage to you, Tanis."

"Since our master of war is fighting on two fronts," grinned Mearith, "perhaps he could use two. Since we're returning to Fugitive to spend the winter, we'll have no need of others."

"Splendid idea, my heart," said Ariel, a smile of true delight on her face. "Trelanth, would you mind spending the winter with these savage farmers?"

"Do I get to play with the Geni seers?" she asked, with a wicked grin.

"Oh yes, of course," Ariel replied with a laugh. "You'll need something to do to pass the time." Just then there was another fuss outside in the square.

"Ho, Kern," called Grace. "You've brought us a goodly number of folks this time. Your queen is inside with Lord Tanis. You go on, we'll see to these folks and the horses."

A moment later the door opened and Kern limped inside, leaning on a woman's arm. With a squeal of delight, she abandoned him and leaped into Tanis' arms. "Dera, let me introduce you. This woman is Queen Ariel, she whom we all serve and to whom we owe our freedom. This woman is Lady Mearith, consort of Queen Ariel. Ladies, this is my beloved younger sister, Dera, companion to Kern the Horseman, my second."

Dera knelt but Ariel took her arm and raised her up. "It's truly a pleasure to meet you, Dera. Tanis often spoke of you, but each time the sadness threatened to consume him. I just don't understand why he gave you to Kern for a leaning post."

"I didn't," Tanis sighed elaborately. "It's all Kern's fault."

"My fault?" said Kern, with feigned innocence. "It's not my fault. She caught me on the ground. I might have escaped on horseback, but I'm lame, can't run. She had me before I knew what was happening."

Dera reached out to lightly caress his cheek. "My poor Kern, so badly maligned, so abused by his companion. Truly it's heartbreaking the fate that's befallen so great a warrior."

This brought a round of laughter at his expense and he shook a finger at her as he blushed then laughed. "My queen," he said, "I have no words to express to you the joy you've given me. You brought me out of the killing shed in Magdan to spend a life with horses, and now my beautiful Dera."

"When did the Pull take you Kern?" asked Mearith.

"As soon as we neared the farm where we found Dera, Lady. I was terrified, for I didn't know what it was, but it was a longing so strong it was painful. Once we reached the forest again I abandoned the horses to the others and approached Tanis who was hugging one of the rescued women. The closer I got the stronger it became, and I prepared myself for death."

Tanis turned fully to his friend. "Kern?"

"From where I stood it looked as though you had claimed her, Tanis. I knew you'd easily defeat me in battle, but I knew I couldn't live without her."

"So, what happened?" asked Ariel, grinning.

"I felt him draw closer," said Dera. "As soon as I realized he was lame and couldn't outrun me, I jumped up and grabbed him. Lady, it was so magical. The instant his arms enclosed me I felt a happiness I could not have believed existed."

"I can understand that," smiled Ariel, "for I have felt the same compelling force at work. I am well pleased for you all."

At that point an Elf burst into the inn. "They're coming, My Lord Tanis."

"Where? How many?"

"Out of Magdan, my Lord, some five hundred men at arms with slaves and wagons. They've been on the road for several days now.

We've cut their numbers some, but there's a mage with them and it's hard to get close. They'll be here in three days."

Grace's eyes were wide, but Tanis patted her shoulder. "Don't worry, Grace, they'll never reach Argar alive. My queen, with your permission I'll be about the task."

"Want some company, Tanis?" grinned Mearith. "Ariel?"

"Oh yes, my heart, we do want to accompany Lord Tanis for this. Trelanth, do something about that mage, will you?"

"Of course, my queen. I'll just be a moment."

While Trelanth sat to meditate and chant, Tanis was issuing orders. "Kern, Dera, get the horses ready, gather the Reavers. Are you certain there are none following you from Shotar?"

"We saw none, my Lord, and we used the tracks for guidance."

"The tracks?" asked Mearith.

"Aye, Lady. Even if a mage hides a man's passage, he still leaves tracks. We always leave a few trackers on our back trail just to make sure we're not being followed by invisible enemies." Mearith grinned and nodded her approval as he and Dera hurried out, Kern leaning on her arm for greater speed.

They were all mounted and waiting when Trelanth came out of the inn to join them. She was grinning with delight. "Trelanth, what did you do?"

"I sent the approaching mage a gift from the forest, my queen."

"Oh?"

"Yes. Each time he now tries to cast a spell his concentration is broken. I placed a bit of poison ivy on his nose. The energy gathered to cast a spell activates it and breaks his concentration. I think he's getting frustrated, and the Elves are reaching them easily now."

Ariel laughed with delight. "Well done, Trelanth. Come, let's go out to join our fellow travelers on the roadway."

They rode through the rest of the day then camped in the trees out of the wind. The next day they found them. "Tanis, you're my general in these lands. Take command and deal with this."

"Yes, my queen. What is my objective?"

"You tell me. What do you want to do here?"

"There are two options, Lady. Option one, defeat them, but send as many as possible back to Magdan alive. Option two is to make sure none ever return. These men have to be a major portion of their men-at-arms. If they don't return Magdan will be weakened considerably."

"I leave the choice to you, my friend," said Ariel.

"Option two it is," he said, his eyes hard as stone. "Lady Trelanth, could you neutralize that damned mage for me please."

"A pleasure, my Lord," she grinned. "Shall I accompany you?"

"By all means," he replied, as he urged his horse forward.

As soon as he was noticed, the Elves who were harrying the riders swept away to the forest. As he rode slowly toward the armed men Tanis pointed to his left, and then his right. Ariel watched with interest as the Reavers parted like water around a boulder and swept out into the field.

Tanis stopped, facing the oncoming riders. He nodded to Trelanth who shot out her arm towards them. The mage fell dead from his horse. Then Tanis spoke, his voice carrying easily across the cold barren fields. "Attention riders, if any of you are farmers willing to work the fields instead of bearing arms to defend the city, throw down your weapons and ride past me. You will find food, shelter, and a welcome in Argar."

"And if we don't?" shouted a voice.

"You will not live to see darkness fall this day." There was some laughing, jeering, and a lot of threats and challenges, but one man broke ranks, threw down his sword and shield, and rode toward Tanis. Slowly three more followed him.

Once they had passed him Tanis called out again. "Any more?" There were none. "So be it." With that he swept his arm into the air then back down.

Ariel sat atop Grimm, watching as the Reavers attacked. The men in armor turned to charge the Elves who attacked from the left, but as soon as they did the Elves attacked from the right. Ariel was amazed as the Elves on the lighter faster ponies swept down on the slower armored horses.

Arrows flew from bows, but the ponies never slowed in their stride as they sped past the armed men at a safe distance. The Elves soon had the riders on heavier horses well spread out. One by one they fell to the rain of arrows.

Nearly half their numbers were down before they managed to regroup near the trees so only one group of Elves could get at them at a time. And then the stallion screamed his challenge and burst from the forest. Grimm sped from the trees and crashed into the mass of lesser horses like a battering ram, Mearith's jet black charger right beside him.

The war horses drove deeply into the enemy ranks and, when they turned to face this new challenge, the Elves redoubled their attack from behind. Ariel and Mearith broke through the mass of armed men and out into the open field, drawing them apart again.

The men at arms broke and tried to flee as Ariel turned Grimm back to face them. He reared up with lashing hooves and screamed his challenge again, then leaped at the armored riders. Their armor was of no use against this monster, and the Elf astride him, although she wore no armor, was still impervious to any weapon. Her bow sang and a man fell even as the beast crashed into their ranks again.

Most of the mounted men were down now, and those who fled the field were pursued and dispatched. Terrified, the Elvish slaves sat huddled in the empty wagons. As the battle ended they were surrounded by Elves, their slave collars removed, then escorted down the road toward Argar.

That night they camped on the empty road. Ariel called Tanis to her and smiled. "My friend, you have exceeded all expectations. Mearith and I will escort the new Bornani to Fugitive and there we will spend the winter.

"We've done it, Tanis. We've established the Road to Elfhome through the mountains, we've set free nearly as many slaves as we did last year, and now we rest while the snow covers the land.

"Keep them bottled up as best you can, my friend. As soon as we're able, we'll return to you with as many warriors as we can put in the field. When the snows leave the lands, we take Magdan and Shotar. Put some thought into that while you rest through the winter."

"Yes, my queen. It will be as you desire."

The next morning Ariel gathered the newly freed Bornani, and with an experienced Elf to guide each one, led them into the forest while Tanis continued along the road back to Argar. "Come, my new friends, my brothers and sisters," smiled Ariel. "Come, let us begin our journey. We will go to Fugitive to spend the winter."

With Mearith riding beside her the Queen led her people into the forest to begin their first steps on the long road home, a place of dreams where they could live free, a dream called Elfhome.

The End

A nd now for a peek at the third chronicle.

A Winter Siege

Third Chronicle in the tale of the Elves of Elandor
(second edition)
by

Prudence MacLeod

IN THE SPRING THAT followed the year of rescue, the Elves came boiling out of the north, driving all before them. The peoples of Elandor fled the villages and farms to seek refuge in the cities, there to hide behind stone walls for protection from the freed slaves and the ancient Borni warriors. A standoff was reached, and then the snows of winter began to fall.

In this, the third Chronicle of the Elves of Elandor, I shall relate some of the hardships and victories of that long and bitter winter.

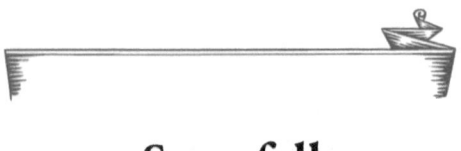

Snowfall

The village of Argar had grown to the size of a town as the Elves brought more and more people there. Lord Tanis used a table at the inn for his headquarters as he conducted the dual sieges of the Geni ruled cities. Both Magdan and the capital city of Shotar were overrun with refugees and besieged by the elusive Elves.

Despite these successes, the young Elvish commander didn't lower his guard, but remained focused. He sat musing softly as he and the mage mulled over the logistics. "So, Eline is taking Ethor and a hundred new Bornani into the mountains to winter at the way stations?"

"Yes, my Lord Tanis. The queen and her lady companion reside at Fugitive now, but with all the new Orcs and Bornani, Fugitive couldn't hold them all. You're concerned?"

"I am, Trelanth, could you take a look and see if Eline made it through before this storm hit?" The mage nodded her head then settled into a meditation. No one disturbed her.

HIGH IN THE MOUNTAINS above the town of Fugitive, two Elves on watch stood beside a tall boulder, nearly invisible to anyone on the trail. They and their companions had worked feverishly through the summer to get the way station ready for the Bornani to use as a rest stop on their long journey north to Elfhone. Now the work was done, and winter was setting in. "What a delightful winter's day! I think something interesting will happen today."

"You sure about that?" grinned his companion. "It rarely ever does."

He winked at her mischievously. "Count on it."

"What would be truly interesting is if that bank of cloud would turn away," she said.

His mood sobered. "Aye, that's the truth of it, but we have another problem. Look coming." There was a dark line of moving figures slowly climbing through the pass. "I wonder, are they friend or foe?"

"I'll go ask them," she chuckled as she stepped out from behind her boulder.

"You be careful, Del."

"I will. If they're unfriendly I'll lead them into the blind canyon. You'll have to drop me a rope to get me out."

"Got it right here." He grinned as she trotted away towards the oncoming mass of people. Del soon recognized the queen's banner, and with a shout of glee, leaped towards them. Within moments she was on her way back at a full run. She didn't even pause as she passed him. "Come on, we've got work to do."

He followed closely as she raced away, heading for the way station.

It was quite late in the year for newly freed Bornani to be making the trek across the mountains. "Get the fires up," he shouted as they neared the station. Several Elves set to work building up fires along the sheltered valley.

Back on the trail, Eline sighed with delight as the land began to level off then slope downwards. In the distance she could see the smoke of many fires rising out of a forested valley. The only thing that could dampen her spirits now was the heavy cloud bank moving swiftly across the sky. She hoped they'd make it to the way station before the storm hit.

At her shout the Elves broke into a run. The land sloped downward and there were trees ahead. The first flakes of snow were dancing in the air as they passed through the trees and found the large encampment beside the stream.

As they neared Eline saw a short, but stout wall surrounded a well spread out grouping of buildings. Fires were dancing in the open spaces and also in some of the shelters. There were three long storehouses and a makeshift forge.

The garrison had been busy, and the storehouses proved to be full. If necessary, the entire group could pass the winter there. They'd have to hunt and forage a bit, but the valley was long and well forested. They would have shelter and food.

The gates were open, and the Elves poured through, spreading out to warm themselves by the fires. As the last one passed the gate ten warriors trotted out into the storm. "Where are they going?" asked Eline.

"Masking your trail," replied Del as she approached Eline and Ethor. "By nightfall your trail will end at the summit. So, Eline, what do you think?"

"I'm amazed. You few have built an entire village in the course of a summer."

"We've worked hard, that's for sure. The idea was to build an empty village, one easily defended, yet one that could be abandoned if need be. There's enough room here for you to spend the winter, and we shouldn't have to do a lot of foraging. It'll be good to have some company."

"Del, we're not all staying. We'll leave about fifty Bornani with you and take the rest on to Station One."

"So, you'll winter there?"

"No, once we drop them off, we'll be coming back through to Fugitive."

"No you won't," replied Del as she looked upwards into the storm. "If this is going to be as bad as I expect, the high pass will be blocked until spring."

"Seriously?"

"Eline, believe me. Look, we've never spent a winter here, but old Vigo has."

"Who's old Vigo?"

"Early the past summer, a small family of Dwarves wandered in, looking to trade and to see what we were up to. He asked if we needed a smith and we readily agreed. He tends the forge and the other three of them tend the storehouses. Auggie is an awesome cook. If she weren't already bonded to Viggo, I might ask her myself."

"I heard that," rumbled a deep voice as a Dwarf couple approached. The woman was chuckling, and he was shaking a finger at Del. "You can just forget about stealing my cook, Elf."

Del introduced them. "Del tells me this storm will block the pass, Viggo, is that right?"

"It is. We've been in this valley for a long time, and I'm actually surprised you made it through. That pass will be blocked until spring now. There's a few deep caverns further down the valley where you could retreat to if the snows get too deep, but otherwise I'd stay clear."

"Oh? Why?"

"Something evil dwells deep in those caverns. Tall and ugly, they are, and hard to kill. You have enough warriors, you'd most likely be able to drive them off, but we couldn't. We left, came out in the open, but most of the clan stayed back to fight."

"So what happened to them?" asked Ethor.

"No idea," he sighed. "It's been a few years now and none of them have ever come out. So, Del tells me there are Dwarves in Fugitive, is that right?"

"Yes, it's true. There's a small clan there now."

"Aye then, perhaps we'll take a trip down there for a visit come summer."

"You'd be welcomed in Fugitive," smiled Eline. "Now, before we start next summer's visiting, tell me what we should do to survive the winter. I'd like to take half our people on to the next way station. What do you think my chances are?"

"Not good, girl. You'd be fine traveling down the valley, but you'd have one more high pass to cross. I expect this storm will block that one too."

"So, we're stuck here for the winter?"

"Aye, it'll be good to have some company, someone to keep Del occupied and out of trouble."

SLOWLY TRELANTH SHOOK off the spell. It had been difficult to see over that distance through the storm. "All is well, my Lord. Eline has reached the first way station, but I fear she'll go no further before the spring comes to the mountains. This storm is a bad one, and it'll block the passes through the peaks."

"But they're safe there, they'll survive the winter?"

"Have no fear, Tanis my friend, Eline has survived and thrived through worse than this."

He sighed and nodded his head. "Then I'm content."

"Tanis, the Spirit Pull isn't the only way we Elves choose a mate, in point of fact, it rarely is. If your heart calls for Eline, perhaps you should speak of it to her?"

Another gentle shake of the head. "No, Trelanth. I'll not speak of this only to have her snatched away to another by the Compulsion two or three years from now."

Wisely, she said nothing more, simply rose and patted his shoulder as she left the room.

Don't miss out!

Visit the website below and you can sign up to receive emails whenever Prudence MacLeod publishes a new book. There's no charge and no obligation.

https://books2read.com/r/B-A-ZKBBB-WGQZC

BOOKS 2 READ

Connecting independent readers to independent writers.

Also by Prudence MacLeod

Children of the Goddess
Lady Blue
Fallen Angel
Lady Justice
Lady Shadow
Lady Seeker
Watcher and Warrior
Shadow Ascending

Children of the Wild
Immortal Tigress
Children of the Wolf
Vampire's Lair
The Hawk and the Wolf
The Oregon Incident
Race the Wind
Heir to the Throne

Elvish Chronicles
Rise of the Queen

The Road Home

Forgotten Worlds
Suvi
Echo of the Past
Survivors
Ship
Fleet
Unite
IGEN
T.E.N.

Nova series
Novan Witch
Assassin of Nova
Beyond Nova
Claimstake
Red Nova

Watch for more at https://www.prudencemacleod.com/.

Telling a story is like knitting a sweater. Start with a ball of possibilities, pull out one small thread and begin. With luck and patience you will create something quite wonderful.

About the Author

On a far off windswept island Jennifer Crandall sits with her dogs and cats creating fantastic stories for all to enjoy. She publishes as JL Crandall, Prudence MacLeod, and Jenni Leigh.

Read more at https://www.prudencemacleod.com/.

www.ingramcontent.com/pod-product-compliance
Lightning Source LLC
Chambersburg PA
CBHW020946180626
46814CB00003B/949